MANDATORY ROLE

JAMES CAMPBELL

Mandatory Role

ISBN: 978-0-9966076-0-5 (print)

MANDATORY ROLE

FOREWORD

This book did not start out as a book but as a haphazard collection of stories. Back in the winter of 2012, I was having a conversation with a friend about retirement and what it might look like. She expressed that she would like to buy a RV and have the freedom to travel wherever and whenever she wished. I laughed and described the image that immediately came to me of her somewhere in Arizona in a 1970s-era Winnebago with no hubcaps, wearing a faded pink terrycloth robe, smoking a cigarette, with multiple cats milling about the RV. She did not find my version very flattering and appropriately directed me to a particularly hot destination. As I hung up and continued my drive from the mountains back to Madison, I concocted the beginnings of this story. The creative process spanned over six months with about twenty emails sent to the characters involved. I was ready to wrap it up and informed my email recipients and fellow characters that the last installment was coming. I had no dramatic ending in mind; it was just time to finish it. At their request, I wrote a proper ending and then went back and tied all twenty stories into one work. It was fun and challenging!

I had several close friends help edit this story and guide me with suggestions and directions. I'm very thankful for their input and implemented the majority of their suggestions.

Putting this collection of stories together, I learned a few good lessons about writing. In particular, it takes a great deal of time, and there are rules for everything. A quote I read somewhere sums it up pretty well: "Writing is not writing; rewriting is writing." So, with many rewrites under my belt, I present to you the adventures of Aubrey, Nathan, and Colby. I hope you enjoy them. Possibly, there will be more stories to tell in the future. You never know where a conversation or an event might lead . . .

James Campbell

CHAPTER ONE

Colby

Cold is too benign a word to describe how frigid and miserable that night was. Fortunately, I was wearing a fleece-lined parka and had about four fingers of warming scotch numbing me from the freezing temperature. Encouraged by the libation, and deciding it would not hurt to have a quick look, I left the comfort of the truck and cautiously approached the RV.

As I stepped up on the solitary step leading inside, it moaned loudly from years of abuse. I paused for a second and then slowly opened the door. I could see nothing and cursed myself for not bringing a flashlight. Entering the RV, an acrid, foul odor filled my nostrils. Immediately, I could see piercing eyes glowing amber from the light seeping under the door of what I assumed was the back bedroom. I had a strange sensation that the floors and walls were moving around me. Suddenly, I felt something brush against my legs!

In a panic, I rushed back to the door, which had closed, and quickly shoved it open. The headlights from my vehicle flooded the room. Cats, at least a dozen of them, were spread out across the RV. The source of the foul stench quickly became apparent. I covered my nose and moved through the RV toward the light coming from the back room. With trepidation, I opened the door. I could not believe what I saw. Lying on the bed, covered in blood, was Aubrey.

—

Her family had contacted me the day I returned home to Georgia after a trip to Europe. I had been driving home from the airport when her mom called. Aubrey, my former girlfriend from way back in high school, was missing and they were frantic to find her. Although Aubrey and I were back in touch, I'd been overseas for the last three weeks and had no idea she had disappeared. While it was not uncommon for us not to talk for a week or so, she rarely went a day without speaking with her mom. For days now, she had not called nor could anyone reach her. They alerted the police, but without any suspicion of foul play, there was not much they could do.

According to her mom, Aubrey had somehow become involved with a movie production that was filming in the area. Mrs. Reese said it was from a connection at work, and for the last few weeks, Aubrey had been driving to a set somewhere near Covington. I assured Mrs. Reese that she was probably fine, but promised to look into it.

After our conversation, I immediately called Aubrey, and her phone went straight to voice mail. The last time we had spoken, everything was great. She was busy painting and restoring furniture. We'd met at my house and shared a bottle of wine, celebrating our birthdays and my upcoming trip to London and Paris, which she'd helped plan. She had never mentioned any involvement in a movie production, and I can only assume it happened while I was away. I began to share Mrs. Reese's concerns after calling a few of Aubrey's friends and co-workers to find they had not heard from her either. I could feel the anxiousness build over the possibility that something bad might have happened to her. After years of being separated from Aubrey, I could not fathom the thought of losing her again.

I walked into my office and sat down at my desk. I opened the top drawer and reached for an envelope that was tucked away in the back. In the envelope were several pictures of Aubrey and me from what seemed like another lifetime. All the memories from so many years ago flooded my mind. They had been the best times of my life.

CHAPTER TWO

Our first encounter had been a fortuitous event at the early age of thirteen. My father had recently joined a hunting club near Jewell, a small East Georgia town set on the banks of the Ogeechee River, midway between Sparta and Warrenton. Aubrey's dad was an original member of the club and eventually became my father's close friend. The day of my first hunt was also the day Aubrey and I met—an occasion far more memorable than the hunt itself. After spending several hours freezing in a deer stand and being quite certain of several lost toes to frostbite, I had quickly let go of my preconceived notion of deer hunting. Envisioning herds of big-antlered deer, I had already picked out a spot on my bedroom wall for the trophy buck I assumed I would harvest. But I did not see the first cotton-picking deer and felt I had been duped!

All the hunting magazines showed pictures of successful, contented hunters posing with record-setting deer. I was extremely disappointed to say the least! I did hear several close shots and was excited to see if anyone had shot one of those magazine bucks. Though I would soon realize that the hunt would not be nearly as exciting—and definitely not as intimidating—as the girl who would soon become a part of my life.

Around noon, after thawing out, I removed myself from an uncomfortable hunting stand located about twenty feet up a hickory tree. I guess I was now considered an official deer hunter. My dad laughed when I informed him of my expectations and severe disappointment. He advised me, as he would many times over the years, that nothing worthwhile comes easy, and everything takes time and patience. We left the woods and drove a few miles to the hunting camp.

Traditionally, after the opening morning hunt, all the members gathered back at a small hunting cabin to discuss and usually over-dramatize what they had seen or shot. We pulled up to see old Jeeps, Broncos, and other big four-wheel drive vehicles parked in front of the cabin. Although perhaps a bit nervous, I was looking forward to meeting the sons of the other members. Being from the city, I was terribly uneducated about guns and hunting and was hoping to make some new friends and learn more about my new hobby. To my surprise, there were no boys in the crowd—just a girl. She was tall (taller than me), lean, and nice looking. She stood next to her father with a Marlin 30-30 rifle slung over her back. I had gazed many times at the Marlin 30-30 behind the gun counter at Kmart and was saving to buy one. I had left my gun in the truck and was glad I had. I was using my dad's paltry single-shot 12 gauge shotgun, and it would have paled in comparison to the Marlin—especially being that it was held by a girl.

She eyed me with suspicion but also with a little curiosity. I'm sure she had been warned about the city boy. We stayed clear of each other, and after lunch, everyone headed back to the woods. I'll have to admit that I did sneak a few glances and was fairly certain that she did as well. Sitting in the deer stand that afternoon, my mind was not totally on hunting.

Later that evening, after leaving the woods, my dad informed me that we were going to drop by one of the club members' houses. We had yet to receive a map of the hunting property, and Mr. Reese, my father's new friend, was making us a few copies. Of course I knew Aubrey was the daughter of Mr. Reese, and with the possibility of seeing her, I spit in my hand and ran it through my hair a few times for good measure.

We rode for several miles through winding back roads before turning up a long tree-lined drive that ended at a large antebellum home wrapped with long, two-story porches. It majestically sat high on a hill over the Ogeechee River floodplain along a section called the shoals. The house was illuminated and looked very inviting. I could imagine that in the daytime, it must have great views of the river. Possibly this new friendship could lead to some future river fishing.

We walked along a pebble sidewalk and up a few stairs to a porch full of rocking chairs and sliding metal gliders. Making our way to the door, Dad announced our arrival with the knock of a heavy brass door knocker shaped like a bird dog. After a few short seconds, the door opened, and there stood Aubrey, but this time not dressed in camouflage and without a gun slung over her back. She had on jeans and a flannel shirt, and her long auburn hair, which had been pulled up in a hunting cap earlier, now flowed freely over her shoulders. Her eyes were the color of emeralds, and without a doubt, she was the prettiest girl I had ever seen. Immediately, I felt flush, and a feeling of embarrassment overcame me.

She very cheerfully invited us in, and my eyes went straight to the floor. I was just beginning to find girls interesting but was not quite ready to engage someone as tantalizing as Aubrey seemed at that moment. We met her parents in the hallway, and after a short greeting, we moved to the den. I did manage to lift my eyes from the floor but only to focus on a large deer head mounted over the fireplace. From the corner of my eye, I sensed her watching me.

"See anything today?" she asked in my direction. There was no escaping her.

"No, I didn't. Did you?" My voice cracked a little and I thought, *Great!*

"No, I didn't either. I was too busy worrying about freezing to death," she answered with the most pleasant smile ever. We both laughed and our nervousness quickly evaporated. We talked until it was time to go. I thought about her all the way home, and I'm not sure she has ever totally left my mind since.

Driving back, Dad, who had perceptively picked up on my newly formed crush, said with a mocking grin, "I guess I won't have to worry about you giving up on all those disappointing expectations and having to hunt alone this year, will I?"

As Mr. Reese and my father became closer friends, we began spending early spring and summer Saturdays at their house in Jewell. About once a month, we would drive down early in the morning and spend the day in the solitude of the country. The river seemed to be the center of entertainment. Aubrey's dad had built a long, winding set of steps leading down to a dock overlooking a swimming hole. I remember a large granite outcrop that rose about twenty feet next to the hole. Aubrey would jump off with reckless abandon and tease me for not having the nerve to do the same. When I finally found the courage, she rewarded me with a kiss—my first kiss. We would

spend many evenings down at the river and entering adolescence on
that dock. Mrs. Reese always worried about Aubrey being around
that old muddy river. I think she should have worried about me!

As fall came, Aubrey was no longer interested in hunting and
moved on to things more important to teenage girls. She joined the
cheerleading squad at the private school just up the road in Warren
County and invited me down one fall Friday night to watch a football
game. Actually, I think her plan was for me to watch her. I was not
yet driving, and Aubrey persuaded Mr. Reese to invite my father to
a local men's Friday night supper.

Soon after Dad and I pulled up, a car load of mutual and older
friends stopped by the house, and I jumped in. Crammed into the
back seat, we headed off to the stadium and arrived right at kick-
off. The first thing I saw was Aubrey in her cheerleading uniform,
and she was stunning. Over the summer, she had grown taller and
matured in ways that teenage boys would certainly notice. I quickly
saw I was not the only one to appreciate the transformation. After
the game, one of the football players approached her and seemed a
little too friendly. I walked right up to Aubrey, put my arm around
her waist, and, with a proprietary smile, introduced myself to the
player. Although not too happy, he seemed to get the message and
wandered off. As we walked back to our friend's car, I felt her arm
slide into mine and pull me close. She looked up with a smile that
said I had done well. Having missed many cues over the years, that
night, I got it right.

After that night, my focus changed from hunting to Aubrey. I
immediately limited my ritual of freezing to death and remaining
perfectly still to the morning hours, and I spent the afternoons and
evenings with her. Dad wasn't too happy about losing his hunting
partner, but he understood, having once been a teenage boy.

My interest in things back home quickly waned. My only thoughts were of the girl in Jewell. I quickly became frustrated with my inability to talk to her as much as I would have liked. My sisters were the dictators of the phone, and I was never allotted more than a few minutes and, even then, only on the odd-numbered days of the week. I protested to my parents, but even they were defenseless against the consortium of the sisters. So I concocted a scheme to overcome this challenge. Late in the evening after our parents and the sisters had gone to bed, we would call each other and talk long into the night. Our plan was that whoever was to receive the call would turn off all the phone ringers in the house. It would usually be her, since the two phone hoarders in my house had a sixth sense when it came to phone use. I would slip down and call her from the basement, where I could not be heard. (In those days, we were not allowed to have phones in our rooms.) Of course, we would remind each other to reset the ringers the next morning.

We got by with this for a month or so until the long distance bills arrived. It seems we had not considered the financial consequences of our growing friendship. Both our parents hit the roof and abruptly put a stop to it. My father made me pay our phone bill and the Reeses'. I can still remember that the total for that month was $97.13. I raked leaves, washed cars in the bitter cold, and reluctantly borrowed money from my sisters to pay the bill. It didn't matter a bit about the money. I would have done it every month just to be able to talk to her.

After a year or so, my father was finally able to convince my mom to visit Jewel. I think her curiosity about my new girlfriend and stories about the Reeses got the best of her. She was pleasantly surprised, and it was not long before she and Mrs. Reese became friends. This was great, because there was no way Mrs. Reese was going to let my mother stay in some run-down shack or the back of a van.

Dad always turned down the invitation to stay at the Reeses' because he didn't want to intrude or put anyone out. Mrs. Reese would almost beg us to stay, and Aubrey and I would hold our breath, hoping he would accept. He never did, leaving us to sleep in the cabin (which was really a shack) at the hunting property or in the back of our old '74 Ford van. I hated sleeping in that van. I remember waking up one night freezing and turning on the heating fan to warm up. I held my hands under that ice-cold air, on the edge of frostbite, waiting for it to get hot. I did not realize the car had to be running to produce heat. Thankfully, those days were over, and it was now assumed that we would stay with the Reeses whether my mom was with us or not.

Relegated to sleeping in the room with my dad (who did not trust a hormonal teenage boy) put a damper on our evenings. After much discord, Aubrey and I finally convinced our parents to allow us to stay up after everyone had gone to bed. Confined to the couch and with every light in the den spotlighting our activity, we would stay up late talking and sneaking kisses. Around midnight, Mrs. Reese would tap a chair leg or something hard on the floor, signaling to Aubrey it was time to go upstairs to bed. Although I ached to do so, I resisted her alluring attempts to sneak me upstairs with her. You had to pass her parents' room to get to hers, and come hell or high water, I did not want to get caught by Mr. or Mrs. Reese. I was crazy about Aubrey and didn't want to take any chances of getting run out of the house at the end of a shotgun.

I so looked forward to the weekends. I finally turned fifteen in May and got my learner's permit. After years of driving with Dad sound asleep in the passenger's seat, I could now legally pilot the car. Of course, he still had to be in the car until I turned sixteen, but he could now rest easier. Being a former race car driver, he loved cars and had taught me to drive at a very young age. At twelve, I had followed him in my mother's 1969 Ford Thunderbird to the tire store about five miles from our house. We had to go through two traffic lights and make several turns. Since I had not yet hit my growth spurt, he placed an Atlanta Yellow Pages on the driver's seat and instructed me to follow him, keep my eyes straight ahead, and look like I was older and knew what I was doing. We did this on several occasions, and needless to say, my mother never knew. The confidence he instilled in me at such an early age paid off in later years when I raced cars myself.

If it's possible to fall in love at fifteen, I'm pretty sure it happened to me. I'd lost all interest in sports and decided to quit the wrestling team because the meets were on Friday nights and sometimes extended to Saturdays. Dad would head down to the hunting land without me, and two weeks would pass without seeing her. Baseball was coming up in the spring and would present a similar challenge. Seeing her only every other weekend was not enough, and I think she felt the same. My coaches were not happy about my decision to quit, nor did my friends in Atlanta approve, but it didn't matter. They could not understand why I had to find a girlfriend so far away when there were so many to choose from closer to home. My buddies were mere boys and, unlike me, had yet to discover the wonderful and powerful emotion of love. Aubrey's friends were not too happy either, but neither of us cared. When she wrapped her arm in mine and rested her head on my shoulder, I was on top of the world, and there was no place I would rather be.

One particular weekend, our whole family piled into the van (which had moon hubcaps, side pipes, and was slightly jacked up in the back—it was the seventies) and off we went to Jewell. Mrs. Reese had called my mom earlier in the week and recruited her to help run the annual Dogwood Festival at Hamburg State Park. My sisters had never been out of the city and had never expressed any interest in venturing anywhere that wasn't in sight of the mall. I suspect they were probably more curious about my new girlfriend than learning the merits of the dogwood tree.

We spent the entire day at the park, and I must say it was probably the best day I'd ever had with my family. Everyone was relaxed and laughing and didn't seem to have a care. That rarely happened in our fast-paced world. Mom and Mrs. Reese worked hard to pull off a successful festival and, after that day, became closer friends. This was good news, because as Aubrey and I looked down the road, it was comforting to know our two families would get along so well. Odd being fifteen and thinking about this, but we had plans, and we weren't getting any younger!

Aubrey and I talked a lot about the future. We were both mid-year in the tenth grade and knew our days in high school would soon be over. I had earned most of the credits needed for the eleventh grade and could probably graduate early my senior year. It stressed us some, the unknown being so close. With my grades and test scores, I had already been pre-accepted at the University of Georgia and had even received interest from Harvard and a few other Northeastern schools. My father encouraged me to explore all my options, but I was dead set on UGA. I had grown up watching the Bulldogs and could not wait to join the Saturday afternoon sea of red and black in Sanford Stadium. I was soon talking to friends about finding a room in Athens.

Unfortunately, Aubrey's situation was a little different. Her mom had attended Georgia College and State University in Milledgeville and, being very active in the alumni association, had her heart set on Aubrey going there. This presented us with a problem. We had assumed we would attend college together, and now it looked as if I would be in Athens and she in Milledgeville.

I'd done the calculations, and it was one hour and twenty-four minutes between the two colleges. We were still about a year and half away from graduating but were already trying to figure out the logistics of leveraging our time.

CHAPTER THREE

O ur birthdays being on the same day, our parents threw
us a party in Jewell when we both turned sixteen. It was
a wonderful Saturday with both our families there to
celebrate. My sisters brought their city boyfriends, who seemed a
bit uncomfortable being far removed from the concrete and asphalt.
After a great picnic on the bluff above the river, we all changed into
our swimsuits and walked down to the dock. We were having a great
time in the swimming hole, and Aubrey somehow convinced my
sisters to jump from the rock perch into the river.

I could immediately see the boyfriends were concerned—not
for the safety of my sisters, but that they would soon be required to
jump as well. Neither saw the merits of launching from a twenty-foot
rock into unknown muddy waters. After a few sneers and taunts
from the girls, pride overtook them, and they found the courage to
take the leap. I had to laugh. It was not so long before then that I had

been in their position. Before the end of the day, I think they must have jumped off that rock a hundred times.

Aubrey and I slipped away and walked up the riverbank hand in hand. After spending the last year and half together, I could not imagine the future without her. At a small cove, we sat on a familiar rock in comfortable silence. Leaning back, she turned toward me with a smile, glowing with happiness and love. I think she was seeing the same future. We made promises to each other that day, and I was as happy as a just-turned-sixteen-year-old boy could be. Later that evening, I gave her a little gold ring with a speck of an emerald, and she gave me a silver necklace with a silver cross.

Shortly after our seventeenth birthday, I received notice that I would have all my high school credits completed by the second quarter of my senior year. I knew I was on track to finish early, and it was time to start thinking ahead. I excelled in math and science and would have all the required courses knocked out by the end of my junior year. There were still a few English and literature classes to complete, and then it looked like I would be ready to start college. When Aubrey and I talked about it on the phone, I could tell she was uncomfortable and a little scared. It would be a big change, and she was having a hard time expressing her feelings. Some things are better discussed in person, so we made plans to talk the following weekend.

I arrived at Aubrey's house early on that Saturday in my new 1968 Mustang convertible. (Well, as they say, it was new to me.) I'd spent the last six months restoring it, and the process had been quite a challenge. Aubrey had been very tolerant and understanding as I constantly complained about something not fitting correctly or costing too much. We jumped in the car and dropped the top, revealing a beautiful May morning with a sky of Carolina blue. We headed out River Road and, by the end of the morning, had kicked up a dust trail on just about every dirt road in Warren County. Aubrey had prepared us a picnic basket, and I parked in a spot overlooking a charming little lake on her uncle's farm.

As we stretched out on our backs on a patchwork quilt, the sun warmed our faces, and the troubles of the world seemed so far away— at least they did for me. I knew what was on Aubrey's mind and was patiently waiting. As the day came to a close, we drove back to the house to witness the setting sun. It appeared to be sinking into the river. Wanting to catch the vibrant colors, we walked down the stairs to the dock.

"Sit," she said as she patted a spot next to her. I could tell by her tone that it was time for our talk. I sat and gave her a tender kiss on her cheek. She beamed with satisfaction, but then got a stern look. "I'm worried about you going to college ahead of me. We've already worked out our plans, and I think we can make it fine if we just stick to them. If you go early, without me, I'm afraid things will change." Aubrey was looking down and twisting a thread of bulrush she had pulled from the river. I could see her concern and need for reassurance.

"Six months will not change anything. Actually, it will be less than that, and then we'll have the whole summer together. I promise there's nothing to worry about. I love you, and I would not let anything get in the way of our future. You just have to trust me that everything will be fine," I said, believing every word. I grabbed her hands and placed them in mine. She slowly looked up, and I could see the anxiety and sadness in her expression. Without speaking, she just stared into my eyes and seemed to see things that were not yet clear to me. She always had that ability. After seconds that seemed like minutes and with tears running down her face, she squeezed my hands and gave me the assurance that she knew I needed. Holding each other tightly, we walked back up the steps from the dock.

Graduating from high school six months early, I hit the ground running for UGA and Athens. I was giving serious thought to just getting a job and waiting on Aubrey, but my parents and the guidance counselor thought I needed to take the opportunity to get a head start. I was one of a small group of students attending college in advance. Most of them were going to Georgia Tech, Georgia State, or the local community college and could still live at home. Several of us were off to UGA and, with the dormitories being full, rented an apartment about two miles from the campus.

Arriving in Athens, we quickly realized that we didn't have time to breathe. They piled the work on us the third day of classes, and my new home became the campus library. It had been so easy in high school, and I'd rarely spent more than an hour or two a day studying. I'm not sure what I was expecting, but I was certainly overwhelmed. My first week in Athens, I barely had any time to talk to Aubrey. When we did talk, all I could tell her was how stressed I was about the workload and all the studying. She was very understanding, but I think she could see the direction things were heading.

Two weeks later, I finally made my way to Jewell and tried my hardest to have a good time. I was distracted for most of the weekend, and she was upset that my mind was elsewhere. I attempted to convince her that she was still my number-one priority, but she didn't believe me. My classes were killing me, and as I explained how much attention they required, it hit me that it was true—she was no longer my main focus. I think by the end of the weekend, I realized she had been right—for the sake of our relationship, I should have waited until the next year. As I made my way back to Athens, my heart was heavy. I knew she was hurting and needed more from me. I had promised her that I would hold things together, but I could feel them slipping away.

I made my best attempt to see her as often as I could, but my life transitioned and I was pulled further into the vortex of college life. It was not the age-old story of cutting the bond of home and partying all night with newfound freedom. I was still dedicated to Aubrey, but with my full course load, we started seeing less of each other, and even the phone calls slowed down. She made all the attempts in the world to keep us together, but I didn't reciprocate. By the time I completed my first two freshman quarters and she finished high school, our relationship had withered to not much more than an occasional phone conversation.

As much as I hate to admit it, I didn't even attend her graduation. I had planned to go, but I was taking summer courses and that Saturday was my first chemistry lab. Strange as it was, we never had any fights or the serious talk with all the clichés about breaking up. What we had together just faded away. She believed that I gave up on us, and maybe she was right. I was contemplating law school and was constantly focused on my GPA.

What a fool I was. I paid too much attention to the wrong things. I ended up with a management degree and by graduation, never wanted to set foot back on a college campus. I thought about her often and would call from time to time while she was still in Milledgeville. She was always polite, but the conversations were cautiously formal. I never had the courage to stand up for what I truly wanted, and it cost me. The day I heard she had a steady boyfriend, it broke my heart. If I could go back in time, I would have waited that extra year, and maybe everything would have worked out like we'd planned. But you can't go back.

While I was attending UGA, my father bought a large tract of land in Warthen, a small, almost non-existent town near Sandersville, Georgia. After thirty-four years with the railroad, his retirement had finally come, and it was time to leave the city behind. He built a quaint cabin in the middle of a hickory hardwood grove surrounded by hundreds of acres of hunting land. Wildlife was abundant and visible most any time of the day. He was happy with his new home, and we no longer hunted the Ogeechee valley.

Jewell, for me, was all but a memory. Mr. Reese and my father remained friends, and I would hear something about Aubrey every now and then. Dad never asked what happened, but I could tell he wished it had been different. We would occasionally talk about her, and he knew how much she meant to me. I always wondered why he never sat me down and shared his fatherly advice on matters of a young man's heart. I guess he figured I had to make my own decisions and it was best to stay out of my affairs. Looking back, I also wonder why I never asked for his advice. I surely could have used it.

Shortly after college, she married the guy she had been dating when we'd last spoken to each other. I remember the awful feeling of despair when I heard the news. I guess on some level I thought she would be there when I was ready. Her marriage didn't last more than a couple years. After the divorce, I heard she disappeared for a while, and any bits of news about her were few and far between. When my father passed, my link to Aubrey passed as well.

In hindsight, I should have moved heaven and earth to find her, but again, my ambitions were my priority. With several friends, I started a logistics company and ended up moving to Winnipeg in Manitoba, Canada. We focused so hard on becoming successful that few of us ever took vacations or visited home. I thought about her often. On cold Canadian nights, I would sit by the fire with a glass of wine and think about those fateful decisions. My mind would drift back to learning the lessons of life by that magical river, so sure of our future. I would wonder where she was and if she ever thought about me and how things might have been. I also wondered if I would ever see her again.

CHAPTER FOUR

L iving mostly in seclusion on the outskirts of Winnipeg, I kind of disconnected from society. I ran the computer logistics part of our company and did most of my work from home. There was an occasional romance, but I never married and never again fell in love. On some level, I felt betrayed by Aubrey and also by myself. I never totally reconciled what happened, and it kept me from moving forward. Thirty years is a long time to hold on to something, but I didn't have much of a choice. You can't lead your heart in a direction it does not want to go.

Having more time on my hands than was healthy, I found several hobbies that took my mind off the life I had left behind in Georgia. During the warm months (which were very few in the cold Northwest), I raced cars and learned to fly airplanes. I'd always had a love for speed and the air, and I took well to both. Following in my dad's successful NASCAR footsteps, I won the regional championship several years in a row. Like my dad, I either won the race or wrecked the car trying. I think he would have been proud. I also quickly flew through my education in flight training, earning my multi-engine, instrument, and commercial rating in just a few years.

But in the cold winter months, there was little to do but watch TV. Every time I turned it on, there seemed to be a global threat from either a third world country or from Mother Nature herself. According to the reports, it was inevitable that we were going to be destroyed by a nuclear bomb from some terrorist group or suffer an EMP strike from the heavens. Either one would lead to a catastrophic economic and social crisis. Prepping was fast becoming in vogue with the paranoid, conspiracy theorists, and I jumped in headfirst. It was not really my nature to be paranoid or obsessed with survival, but hell, I had nothing else to do and it involved blowing things up.

After becoming a regular at the local military surplus store, I was approached and invited to join a little survivalist group in the Red River Valley town of Stony Mountain. I had no idea what to expect at my first meeting but quickly found a kinship with the weird group of guys. Most of them were loners like me and possessed a high IQ. Over the years, I learned more than I ever should have about protecting yourself and your environment. Little did I know that one day those skills and knowledge would prove to be most valuable.

After close to thirty years in Canada, it was time to come home. We sold the company to a large national transportation firm, and I eagerly entered early retirement. It took me a few weeks to load up a container with all my special supplies and say goodbye to my unlikely group of friends. I'd purchased my dad's farm from my sisters years earlier, and being that the house was fully furnished, I sold most of my furniture with the house in Winnipeg. I was excited and nervous about moving back. I had not kept in touch with anyone from my past and wondered what direction they had taken and where they'd ended up—and, of course, I wondered about Aubrey.

Arriving in Warthen, I settled in at the farm with a rush of memories. I had not thought too much about my dad since he passed away in 1995, but being back at home changed that. The house was exactly how I remembered it from so many years before. I could count on one hand the times that I had visited the farm since moving to Canada. I think I believed the old adage "Out of sight, out of mind" would keep thoughts of the past at bay, and for the most part, it had—but not anymore. I felt more alone at the farm than I had in Canada. Maybe being closer to the things that really mattered changed my perspective. Wanting to no longer suffer in self-loathing or pity, I decided the place needed some happy faces. I took a visit to the local animal shelter and acquired two redbone coonhounds that had been previously dropped off at the local dump.

Hannah and Savannah had a new home, and I had a couple of new friends. I spent the next year repairing the three houses and sheds and taking on a few special projects. I had all my supplies from my previous life gathering dust and accomplishing nothing by sitting in the storage container. It took a lot of planning and about a month or two of tedious work, but I was satisfied with the result. The Red River Valley boys would have been proud.

Most days I stayed busy outside until dark, but the nights became long and I found myself becoming overcome by loneliness. The company of the floppy-eared dogs went a long way, but one-sided conversations could only go so far.

A few days later, on the way back from Atlanta, I stopped off for lunch in the town of Madison. I remembered it from my youth and was impressed with all the old Southern-style antebellum homes. I felt immediately lured in by the charming town and, after a bottle of wine that night, decided to think about moving there. With the help of an overzealous real estate agent, I signed a contract for a house the next week. For someone who had been complacent for the past thirty years, things were getting more exciting by the day.

I moved to Madison and was there barely a month before my fateful encounter with Aubrey. Being new in town, I began receiving invitations to many of the town's social events. Southerners are famous for being hospitable, and I was enjoying getting to know the people of Madison. You're only new in town for so long, and I was taking full advantage of it. My next-door neighbor was unknowingly responsible for setting up the serendipitous rediscovery. He had saved me when I was moving in by helping me carry several heavy items of furniture up two flights of steps. I had arranged to meet a friend at the house to help me unload, but he never showed. (He later said he misunderstood and thought it was another day. It's odd because he sure had a sharp memory when it came to remembering the dates of our hunting and fishing trips.)

To show my gratitude to my neighbor, I gave him a bottle of 2007 Wente Vineyards Southern Hills Cabernet Sauvignon from the Livermore Valley. I had been out to the region just before retiring and had sent home a couple of cases. Taking note of my love of wine, he insisted I attend the Madison wine club. The following Thursday, he and his wife were hosting that month's event and asked me to bring a bottle of the Wente and tell the group about the wine and my visit to the vineyard. So a few days later, with an appetizer and wine in hand, I walked next door, and that night my life changed in ways I would have never expected.

Aubrey was the first person I saw when I walked into the room. I could not believe my eyes. She was just as beautiful, if not more, than the last time I'd seen her. We recognized each other immediately, and I'm sure she was just as surprised. We locked eyes for a few seconds before Kurt, my neighbor, greeted me in the foyer. I wanted to go straight to her, but the house was full and the host and his wife graciously began introducing me to the wine club members. I was stuck in conversation, and Aubrey kept her distance and stayed on the opposite side of the room.

It was not long before Kurt announced we would begin introducing our wines. I was nervous as hell when it came my turn. I had just seen, for the first time in almost thirty years, the only girl I ever truly loved. The last thing on my mind was introducing wine. I told myself to just stare at the back of the room and I could get through it. When I looked up, she was in the back of the room, directly in my line of sight. We made eye contact, and I just stood there. Everyone was silent, waiting for me to speak. I don't know how long it lasted, but the silence was broken when Kurt loudly cleared his throat. I snapped back into the moment and dribbled out something about the wine. It was clearly an uncomfortable moment, and I'm sure everyone just assumed it was a case of stage fright.

When I finished my spiel, I looked for her, but she was gone. She had slipped out before I could approach her. I considered asking my neighbors about her—but was not sure I wanted to hear what they might say. What if she was happily married? I walked back to my house with a feeling that was hard to describe, maybe a sense of excitement overshadowed with a touch of dread.

A couple of days later, I wandered into the antique market where she worked. I'm not sure if she thought I had sought her out or just ambled in, but I could tell by her smile that she was pleased. The first thing I looked for was a wedding ring and quickly saw that she was not wearing one. After saying a silent, "thank you, lord," I explained to her that I was there to look at a coffee table made out of an antique door.

Someone in town had told me about a lady that made them and said she worked at the antique market. By her expression, I immediately knew it was her. It appeared that fate had again brought us together. She showed me a few of her pieces, and they were exactly what I was looking for. I purchased one under the condition she would help me place it in my new house. That actually sounded absurd, since it was just a matter of putting it in front of the couch.

If my miserable attempt at getting her to come over was obvious, she didn't let on. She agreed, and we slowly began rekindling our friendship. After about three months and several turned-down invitations, she finally took me up on an offer to prepare dinner. I remembered she liked wild game and grilled an entrée of dove wrapped in bacon. I was tempted to find something resembling an olive branch and hang it from the bird, but I didn't want to press my luck! All went well that night, and as she was leaving, she gave me a hug that I would not have traded for a million dollars.

After that evening, we began to spend a little more time together. Mostly, it was just the two of us and only at my house. I would ask her to accompany me to functions and events, but rarely did she accept. There was an unspoken awkwardness that we could never seem to overcome. We enjoyed cooking, exploring wines, and talking about books—but we never talked about the old days. Amazingly, two years after reconnecting, we had never spoken about anything from our youth. She never asked me about my life in Canada and never mentioned her marriage or life afterward. I attempted to broach the subject a few times, but she always circuitously led us to another topic. It was clear that she had left the past in the past, and I did not want to push her into talking about it. I hoped one day to be able to discuss those early days and tell her I had made the biggest mistake of my life in choosing college over her. I wanted her to know how much I regretted not following through on our promises and letting my own selfish ambitions ruin a wonderfully planned future. After seeing her at my neighbor's wine event, I realized what I already knew: that my feelings for her had never died and were as strong as ever.

At the time I learned that she was missing, I still hadn't found the courage to tell or show her for fear that she might not feel the same. After all, why should she open her heart or ever trust me again? I would have given anything for another chance—but that was a matter for another time. My only thought at that point was to find her.

CHAPTER FIVE

After a long, tiring day, I begrudgingly got dressed for wine club. Usually I looked forward to our monthly meeting, but after my long flight and being preoccupied with Aubrey, I was not up for it. One of my pilot friends was hosting the night's event, and having previously committed, I decided I should attend. At least I could talk flying and distract myself for a few hours. I'd spent the afternoon making phone calls, attempting to find information on Aubrey's whereabouts—but to no avail. I was beginning to get a strange feeling that something really might be wrong.

Arriving at wine club, I was immediately handed a glass of pitiful-tasting white wine. The warm-up wine, as I call it, is usually the cheapest sold at the wine store and serves as filler until the good wine is introduced. I smiled and thanked the host and found the first convenient spot to ditch the glass. I spied a bottle of scotch on a nearby bar and snuck over and poured a few fingers in a clean wine glass. It was a bottle of eighteen-year-old Macallan and probably cost more than all the wine there combined. I smiled as I sniffed the wonderful smell of oak and peat, knowing no one would ever know I was breaking the rules. I milled around the room and made small talk. I did enjoy the camaraderie, but it could be somewhat superficial. Aubrey joked and called it "gossip club." She would later appreciate the irony of the evening.

Being six hours ahead of everyone in the room, I sat down in an overstuffed chair and tried my best to stay awake. I figured I needed to stay a little while longer to avoid being rude. My Southern upbringing would produce profound results. Sitting there half asleep, I overheard Aubrey's name in a conversation between two ladies

"Did you hear the latest on Aubrey Reese?" one of them asked. I perked up and tried not to make it obvious that I was intently listening.

"No, I haven't," the other said, trying to mask her enthusiastic curiosity.

"Well, from what I heard, she took a temporary leave from her job at the antique market to become a movie star," the lady reported with delight.

"Really? What is the movie? Is it being filmed here in Madison?" her companion asked.

"No, it's some kind of low-budget film, and I heard the set was in Porterdale."

"You don't think it's one of 'those' kind of movies, do you?" the lady asked in a hushed tone while making those ridiculous air quotation marks.

"I don't know, but she's gone missing, and the last place anyone saw her was in Porterdale, poor thing! If I find out anything, I will let you know."

They walked off proudly, having had their fill of gossip, and I had my first lead. I politely excused myself and headed back to my home in Saye Creek. Before going to bed, I decided to pour another scotch and sip it on the back porch. My house is a reproduction of a raised Charleston cottage with big porches on the front and rear. Those porches have been host to many thoughts, and that night my thoughts were on Aubrey.

I plopped down in an old metal rocker from the 1950s I'd found in Jewell and recently restored. Driving the dirt roads around the Ogeechee River Valley in my old farm truck was one of my favorite weekend pastimes. I would load up the dogs, and we would set out on an afternoon adventure full of sights and smells. On one particular trip, I noticed the rocker and several chairs on the front porch of an old dilapidated house located by the river. Aubrey and I had parked next to that old house many times to access a trail that led to a small beach. After many attempts, I finally caught the owner at home and stopped to make an offer. I think she thought I was nuts offering so much, but the price of memories can be high. I spent about six months refinishing the rocker and thought about Jewell every time I sat and rocked—and thinking about Jewell was thinking about Aubrey.

After a few minutes outside, I began to shiver from the cold, but the chill aided in clearing my mind. I sat for a few minutes and finished the mind-warming drink. My plan was to go to bed and get a fresh start in the morning, but I could not get her off my mind. Feeling a sense of urgency, I decided to take the twenty-minute drive to Porterdale and look around.

Arriving in Porterdale, I had no idea where to start and just took one road at a time. The town was asleep, and I'm sure on a night like this, to anyone awake, I stuck out like a beacon. The expedition was probably not a good idea with the evening's wine and scotch, but I continued nonetheless. Searching my way past the mill and about a half a mile south of town with no luck, I decided it would be better to come back and search during the day. The temperature gauge on my mirror glared thirteen degrees and the Weather Channel reported a sixty percent chance of freezing rain. I could already see a light coat of sleet forming on my windshield. It would not be good to get stuck out there if the icing were to pick up. Wherever Aubrey was, I prayed she was indoors and warm.

The last street on my left was Wheat Street, and with a little hesitation, I decided to make one last run before heading back to Madison. The road was dark, deserted, and just had a malevolent feel. I reached the end and was turning around in an old abandoned drive when it appeared. Parked at the end of the road was a dilapidated RV that looked to be from the 1970s. With a strong feeling of foreboding, I eased my way forward. Aubrey's Jeep Cherokee was parked beside the RV, and I knew she must be there. Everything was completely dark, with the exception of a dim light coming from the rear of the RV. Something was not right, and I had a sinking feeling in the pit of my stomach. I flicked the headlights several times and sounded the horn. For a quick moment, it looked like something moved near the front door, but nothing was there. Cautiously, I exited the truck and approached the door to knock, but it was already ajar, so with apprehension I slowly entered . . .

Aubrey was covered in blood, and her hair was a red, twisted mat hung over the bed. I was stunned with fright and couldn't move. She wasn't moving either. I could hear her labored breathing and knew she was at least alive. Whoever had done this appeared to be gone, and from the looks of her, she had been left for dead. As I stood there, feeling the danger of the situation all the way to my bones, my mind was flooded with questions—but they would have to wait. I had to move! Having no idea if the assailants might be coming back, I needed to get her out of the RV. I also didn't know the extent of her injuries, but at this point, it didn't matter.

Before I could complete that last thought, she flew off the bed like she had been hit with lightning. In one fluid motion, she grabbed a small handgun from the floor and stuck it under my chin. How I noticed so fast I haven't a clue, but the gun was a Walther PPK.380. It was a gun made famous by James Bond, and it was one that I had given her! The thought crossed my mind that I was about to be shot by my own gun. The rage and fury in her eyes blinded her from recognizing she was about to shoot her friend, or whatever you might call me. We obviously had a few unresolved issues, and I desperately hoped this was not going to be the method of resolution. I called out her name the best I could with a gun shoved at my throat. "Aubrey!"

I sensed recognition in her eyes, and she took a deep breath and removed the gun. I let out the breath that I had taken when I first entered the room. With it being apparent that we didn't have time for questions, she grabbed my hand and pulled me though the RV. The truck's headlights illuminated the room, and there appeared to be more cats than I had previously thought. They must have been satisfied with their living arrangement since they were still hanging around through all the commotion. Halfway to the door, Aubrey stopped quickly to remove a small military-style bag from under a hinged bench table that also served as a seat. With little regard for the cat that occupied the space, she grabbed the animal by a leg and flung it my way. I barely had time to dodge the cat as it flew inches over my head and collided with the door. With the bag in hand, and just behind a herd of scared cats, we exited the RV.

She ran toward the truck, and I was a quick step behind her. As we reached the rear of the truck, I asked what was happening. She didn't reply and removed something from the bag. It was a small device that resembled a TV remote. She handed it to me and very calmly said, "Push the red button in the middle."

I started to ask why but decided against it and pushed the button. As I was being knocked to the ground, my mind was registering the huge explosion that followed along with the consuming fireball. We quickly rolled under the truck to escape the hail of debris. As soon as RV parts stopped falling, I yelled, "Get in." After that little stunt, I realized she was not as injured as I had thought.

—

I spun the wheels as we turned south onto Georgia Highway 11, keeping half my attention on the road and half in the rearview mirror. I was trying to process what had just happened and could not imagine what she might be involved in. I did, however, have a good idea of how she had blown up the RV.

"So what in the hell have you gotten yourself involved in? Those were propane bombs, weren't they? Let me guess. You had at least four twenty-gallon tanks wired with blasting caps and Semtex-10, didn't you?" I asked as a flow of adrenaline coursed through my veins. She just sat there staring out the window, ignoring me and refusing to answer my questions.

"Why would you need to blow up the RV—and, might I add, your Jeep along with it?"

No reply.

"By the way, I know who you got the stuff from." It was apparent I was talking to myself. Her mind was miles away. After a couple of minutes, I could hear her exhale.

"I knew it would come to this," she said. "I just didn't expect them to find me so soon."

"Who are *they*?" I quickly asked. She buried her head in her hands and massaged her temples.

"It's a long story, and I'll answer all your questions later. Just please get me out of here."

"All right. I'll wait, but our next stop is the hospital."

"No hospital," she said with a defiant tone.

"You need medical attention, and that's where we're going unless you have a better idea," I said with a flare of attitude to match hers. After just having saved her from God knows what and being tricked into blowing up the RV, I at least deserved some cooperation.

"Don't you have some doctor friend?" she asked. The only doctor I knew was located in Thomson, a town about two hours away. He was a pilot friend, and I was fairly certain he'd flown to New Orleans for a medical conference. I had no idea where to go and was trying to think of someone who might have experience in situations such as this. For some reason, Nathan Roark popped into my mind, and I knew he was in Madison from an earlier conversation. Nathan and I had become good friends over the last year or so. We had actually met at the Madison wine club and found we both had a streak for adventure. Nathan would tell stories about exciting third-world trips and I would describe the adrenaline rush from racing cars at high speeds. Little did I know that any of our past experiences would pale in comparison to what was about to happen.

"We're going to Madison to find Nathan Roark," I said.

"That guy from wine club? He's not a doctor! I don't want some creep from wine club putting his hands all over me," she said.

"He's not a creep, and I think he can help us. He was in Vietnam, and I'm betting he has experience tending to wounds like yours. Plus, he's a good friend, and I trust him. If he can't help us, maybe he can lead us to someone who can."

Aubrey was getting wearier by the minute. She closed her eyes and leaned her head against the window. I grabbed her arm and shook her.

"You can't go to sleep. You might have a concussion, and they say never go to sleep with a head injury."

She opened her eyes for just a second and then closed them once again. "I'll take my chances. At this point, not waking up wouldn't be such a bad thing."

It took about twenty-five minutes to drive back to Madison. I parked the car in a dark, out-of-the-way spot and helped Aubrey walk the few blocks to Nathan's condo. It would have made more sense to park in front, closer to the condo, but there had been enough surprises for one night, and it was possible that we could have been followed. Aubrey complained the whole time about having to walk so far. I took that as a good sign. We made our way up the elevator and down the hall to the door. I hadn't thought to call on the way and could only guess how Nathan would react when he answered the door. Not only were we dropping by at a late hour, but we were bloody to boot.

After I knocked heavily on the door a few times, Nathan answered and did not seem surprised. He took immediate action and helped Aubrey to the couch.

After some uncomfortable hesitation, he slowly began to unbutton Aubrey's blouse. I could see beads of sweat forming on his brow. Noticing that he seemed to be struggling with the task, I offered my assistance. Of course, I was very concerned with Aubrey's medical condition and felt I needed to do more than observe. As I reached down to assist with the third button, Aubrey opened her eyes and dryly said, "My injury is to my head, not my breast."

We looked at each other, quite embarrassed. With the blood covering her shirt, Nathan had naturally assumed her chest was the main site of her injuries. Red faced, we turned our attention to Aubrey's head and pulled back her hair. She had a huge gash and a nasty bump on the side and back of her head. The blood had clotted, and her hair was a sticky, tangled mess. Nathan wanted to cut it to better examine the wound, but the look on Aubrey's face said that was not going to happen. Head injuries often appear worse than they are due to heavy bleeding. Although her wounds did not seem to be life threatening, Aubrey was having double vision and suffering from an incredible headache. It was apparent she needed an MRI or a CT scan, but she would not hear of it.

Nathan did the best he could with the resources he had. He cleaned the wound, applied an antibiotic cream, and wrapped it with a bandage. He checked the medicine cabinet and found an old bottle of Lortab. He gave Aubrey a pill with a glass of water and led her to the guest bedroom, again advising her that she should not go to sleep.

She paid us no attention and stretched out on the bed. Within minutes, she had found temporary refuge.

Nathan and I returned to the den, and he had a thousand questions, for which I had very few answers. The first and obvious was, *What the hell was happening?*

I filled him in on what little I knew. He let out a small chuckle when I told him the part about being tricked into dispatching the RV. We tried to come up with ideas about what Aubrey might be involved in, but they were all just guesses and we would not know until she woke up.

When she did, it was with a stir and a fright. It was pitch dark in the bedroom, and I'm sure she had no recollection of where she was. Nathan and I had dozed off on the couches and were startled awake by the commotion. She was yelling, screaming, and knocking things over, trying to find the light and the door. We should have known better than to turn out the light.

We ran back to the bedroom, opened the door, and switched on the light. She was across the room with her hands on the wall, trying to get out. I felt really bad, and I'm sure Nathan did as well. She looked scared, and who wouldn't have been? I ran over and tried to comfort her. I wrapped my arms around her and told her she was safe and everything would be all right. Who the hell knew if everything would be all right, but it's what you say in times like that. She was shaking, and I held her closer and tighter. After a few seconds, she calmed and we eased our way back to the kitchen. She was pale from the blood loss and still had a terrible headache, but her vision had returned to normal. I found some orange juice in the refrigerator and poured her a tall glass. We gathered around the breakfast table, Nathan and I anxious to hear her story. She took a sip of juice, then a deep breath, and began to talk.

"Colby, I think it was the Thursday before you went to Paris..."

CHAPTER SIX

Aubrey

That's when I began my story. I was about to blow their minds. I started with my monthly trip to the Decatur Antique Market, where I spent the whole day trying to find bargains. Late in the day, I decided to walk outside for a break. I sat down at a picnic table and was drinking a bottle of water , trying to decide what to buy, when a tall man asked if he could join me. Several tables around me were empty, so it seemed like an odd question. I hesitated, then reluctantly told him, "Sure." He sat down a few feet away, on the opposite side. After a few minutes of appearing to be studying the antique-sales program, he cleared his throat and asked if he could ask me a question. I was busy and short on time, but again said, "Sure."

He assured me he was not trying to pick me up or ask me out and only wanted to know about antique shops in the area. I told him I was not actually from Decatur and didn't know of any. He then revealed he was filming a movie east of Atlanta and wanted to find some antique props a little closer to the set.

Hearing "east of Atlanta," I asked him where. He said it was in a small town called Porterdale, near Covington. Porterdale is not far from Madison, and I was thinking this could be a great opportunity for some big sales. The winter had been slow, and the movie production company could be our saving grace to finalize a challenging year. I told him our little community was the antique capital of Georgia and that he could find whatever he needed at our antique market in Madison. He seemed like a nice guy, and I told him where I worked and to come by and see if we had anything he could use.

A few days later, he showed up at my work with a list of items needed for the production. We spent several hours in the market loading up all available handcarts with antiques. I think he bought every item in the market that was circa 1950. According to the owner, it was the biggest sales day in the market's history. The next day, he came back and bought more stuff and asked if I could take him to several of the other antique shops to complete his list. Usually, we don't steer customers to other antique shops, but we had nothing left to sell. The owner practically shoved me out the door to assist our new best customer.

I took him across town to the Madison Markets, and it turned out to be a banner day for them as well. At the time, I had no idea what kind of movie they were filming but was thinking it must be something special to have what seemed like such a big budget. We finished our shopping spree, and he issued instructions to his crew to load up the antiques in a cargo-type moving truck. I had driven my Jeep and was fishing in my purse for my keys when he put his hand over mine. He told me he could not thank me enough for helping him find the props for the movie and that he did not know what he would have done without me. I felt a bit unsettled by his touch but figured it to just be a well-meant gesture. He then said he had a proposition for me. He must have read my expression and assured me it was not *that kind* of proposition.

He invited me to visit the movie set the following week. He said they had a small role that had yet to be cast, and that after being around me for a few days, he thought I would be perfect for the part. Before I could decline, he held up his hands and said, "I know what you are thinking, and it's not that." He said it was more of a documentary about a local figure than a movie. His company specialized in historic events and filmed all over the country. Filming was to start Monday, and he asked me, "What would it hurt to ride over and check out the set?" He handed me a business card with the address of the set printed on the back.

Colby interrupted me. "Don't tell me you actually fell for that?" he asked.

"Well, hell," I said, "it's not every day someone comes along and asks if you want to be in a movie. I'd been around him for a few days, and everything seemed legit. Everyone at the antique market had met him, and I saw no harm in driving to Porterdale on Monday and checking it out."

"So what happened to cause you to leave home and end up at the trailer in Porterdale?" Nathan asked.

"Well, that's where things start to get interesting, and you're not going to believe the story I'm about to tell," I said.

But I had to wait to tell it.

Chapter Seven

Colby

There were three loud reports as the front door came crashing in. The noise was deafening and temporarily paralyzed our movements and thoughts. Fortunately, we were in the breakfast area. The front door opened to a hallway facing the den, and had we been there, we would've been caught dead in their sights.

I immediately realized we were in big trouble. Nathan's home is a condo located on the top floor of the James Madison Inn. There is only one entrance, therefore, only one exit. Making matters worse, the condo was quickly becoming engulfed with tear gas.

My confused mind was slowly starting to process what was happening. When I say slowly, I mean seconds when it needed to be split seconds. I had no idea who these people were and how they had located us, but we needed to move fast!

"Quickly," Nathan yelled and motioned for us to follow. He ran over to a door facing West Washington Street. The tear gas had not yet reached us and was momentarily acting as a shield, blocking our position. Nathan jerked opened the door, revealing a small balcony. Apparently, part of the fire-safety exit plan was to have a rope ladder readily available and stowed on the balcony. This fire-safety plan saved our lives.

Nathan fastened the rope ladder to the balcony rail with two clevis hooks and flung it over the side. I could hear our pursuers enter the room, and there was no time for instructions. Aubrey shot down the rope, and Nathan was right behind her. Things were happening so fast, and I found myself standing there alone.

"Colby, now!" Nathan yelled.

I could feel the concussion of the bullets as they flew past my head and destroyed the glass panel in the open door. I launched off the balcony and grabbed the ladder with desperation. Nathan and Aubrey were waiting below. As I hit the ground, they quickly pulled me from the sidewalk as a hail of bullets hammered the space I had just occupied. Using the buildings as a cover, we ran east along Washington Street.

Fortunately, I'd had the foresight to position the truck a few blocks to the southeast, near the entrance to a cemetery. I yelled for them to follow me, and we headed in that direction. As anomalous as it sounds, the closer we got to the cemetery, the further we got from the clutches of death.

We stayed on the side streets to avoid the streetlights and cut in front of a catering business and Madison Markets. With the aid of some low-voltage landscape lights, I located a path leading into the cemetery. I'd parked the truck at the Kolb Street entrance, and that was our destination. We followed the bowl-like trail for about fifty yards and turned back east at an old gravesite from the Civil War. We ran another seventy-five yards and reached the gate.

Aubrey was feeling her injuries and had to be helped into the back seat of the truck. Nathan jumped into the passenger seat as I started the engine. Not thinking to bypass the interior automatic light function, we sat there like a lit-up billboard. I turned off the dome lights and backed down Kolb Street, expecting the worst. I knew the shooters had seen the direction we were headed, and I fully expected bullets to come flying our way. So far, I didn't see any sign of our pursuers. Maybe we'd just gotten lucky.

I headed down Academy Street and made my way over to Dixie Avenue. My goal was to escape town in the direction of Rutledge. There would be little traffic, and we would be able to see and get away from any approaching cars. It was dark and quiet with no cars in sight. After we had driven a few miles out of town and it appeared we were not being followed, I pulled the truck onto the shoulder of Crawley Road.

For the second time that evening, I was escaping unknown villains with no destination in mind. We took a collective breath and continued to scan the road for traffic.

"They're not following us, but I'm not sure how we managed it. Anyone have any ideas where to go?" I asked.

"I have no idea, but Madison is obviously not an option. We have to keep moving; they seem to be one step behind us," Nathan said.

I sat there thinking about what he had just said, and nothing made sense. They may have gotten lucky and found Aubrey, but how did they know about Nathan or me? Neither of us had entered the picture until a few hours before. How they had known we were in Nathan's third-floor condo was a mystery. It's almost like they had known our location and taken their time to plan the attack. That's when it hit me!

"Aubrey, where did you get the remote that blew up your trailer?" I asked.

"From my bag." She held up the small military-style bag she had grabbed from under the table.

"Let me see it."

She handed me the bag and I began to remove and inspect each item. When I retrieved a certain object, I knew the answer immediately. It was an iPod. Everyone knew Aubrey did not go anywhere without her music. I removed the back cover, and there it was. A small GPS locator chip was blinking out our position. I held it up so Aubrey and Nathan could see the chip.

"Son of a bitch!" Aubrey yelled. "That's how the bastards knew where I was."

I knew they must be right behind us, and I had an idea.

"Let's get moving. I want to make a quick stop in Rutledge before we leave town," I said. As we drove into Rutledge, I explained to Aubrey and Nathan what I was planning.

I had read in the paper that it was "cowboy rapper" night at the local nightclub. As we drove through the packed parking lot, we could hear the loud music thumping from inside the building. I parked in a dark spot toward the back of the bar and told Nathan and Aubrey I would be right back. I quickly made my way along the rear of the building and found what I was hoping to find. The back door to the kitchen was slightly ajar, and I followed the line of light to the entrance. I slowly opened the door and could feel the heat coming from the ovens. I peeked in and did not see anyone in the room. Removing the iPod from my jacket, I slid it under the three-compartment sink. I locked the door and shut it as I eased my way out and ran back to the truck. It would have been interesting to hang around and see how our perpetrators mixed with the patrons of the nightclub, but we were leaving Morgan County far behind, and I knew just the place to make our escape.

—

We arrived in Warthen a couple hours later, and I was exhausted. Nathan and Aubrey were fast asleep, and I could barely keep my eyes open. I made my way down the mile-long dirt driveway and pulled up to the house.

The place held a lot of wonderful memories and was my refuge from trouble and stress. After my father passed away, my sisters and I had kept the land for a few years, but with me living so far away, it had not made much sense to hang on to it. We'd almost sold it to the farmer who owned the land adjacent to it, but after many sleepless nights, I decided to buy out my sisters and keep it. I had just started my business and had to scrape and borrow enough money to buy my family's interest. But I never regretted the decision, and it was a constant reminder of my dad. It had been our place of bonding, and sometimes I thought I could feel his spirit dropping in for a visit. The thought that I might be inviting or bringing trouble was a little disconcerting.

As we pulled up to the house, Hannah and Savannah greeted us with barks and wagging tails. We failed to match the dogs' enthusiasm and marched stiffly and slowly toward the house.

Aubrey was holding her head and not looking well. Nathan and I helped her into the house and to the back bedroom. I pointed Nathan toward a side bedroom and headed to my own room. Our adrenaline was spent, and we had nothing left.

Late in the morning, I awoke from a dream, startled and shaken. In my dream, Dad and I were furiously chopping and stacking firewood. We had produced a large pile but did not let up. I could clearly see his worried, intense expression as he stared at the clouds, which were dark, grey, and fast moving.

"Hurry up, son; the storm will be here soon," he said. The weather service had predicted the worse ice storm in twenty-five years. Warnings had been issued that power in the rural area could be out for days, if not weeks. Dad looked at me and continued, "Times like this, you never want to be unprepared. Understand?"

"Yeah, Dad, I understand." What I really understood was the meaning of the dream. My father had passed away eighteen years earlier, and I rarely dreamed of him. It was time to put together a plan.

It was well after noon, and the house was still quiet. We had arrived only five hours earlier, and I felt like I could sleep all day. Sitting up in bed, I played over in my mind the events of the previous night. I had never been shot at and realized that just a few inches closer and I would have never made it out of Nathan's condo.

Glancing out the window, I saw that all seemed well. So far, we seemed to have escaped—but for how long? Jumping out of bed, still wearing my clothes from the previous evening, I made my way to the kitchen. From the refrigerator, I pulled enough "just-out-of-date" items together to make breakfast. The smell of the sausage and eggs must have coaxed my two guests from their sleep. They both entered the kitchen looking like death warmed over. Aubrey's neck and the right side of her face were black and blue. I assumed she had not yet looked in the mirror, and of course, I did not mention it. Nathan just looked like hell.

"Hope you two are hungry," I told them.

"Coffee," Aubrey said.

"Bourbon," Nathan said with a slight smile.

I made us all plates and served Aubrey coffee and Nathan his faux bourbon in the form of apple juice.

We sat at the long dining room table and ate in silence. I'm sure we were all processing the past evenings' events and wondering what would happen next.

I heard Aubrey start to cry and looked up to see her hands covering her face.

"I'm so sorry to have gotten you both involved in this. I just want to go home," she said as her sobbing picked up. Nathan got up and moved to the chair beside her. Putting his arm around her, he told her everything was going to be all right. It sounded better coming from him. I still don't think any of us actually believed it, but it was nice to hear. I'm sure he was thinking how thankful he was that his wife was safe visiting their boys in Florida—or so he hoped.

After we finished our breakfast and had a few minutes of silence, I asked Aubrey if she felt like continuing the story. I was becoming very anxious to know who was tracking us down and trying to kill us. I asked her to take her time and give us all the details she could.

CHAPTER EIGHT

Aubrey

My head was killing me, but I'd nearly gotten Colby shot—
and his friend Nathan too. The least I could do was tell
them what was going on. I dabbed away some tears and
picked up where I'd left off.

I'd shown up on the set the following Monday and was met by
Mark McClure, the man from the antique market. I was glad to see the
set was outside and not inside some scary warehouse. Mark walked
me around the set and explained what the documentary was about.
The story line was about a man named Alan Margolin.

Margolin, back in the 1950s, became the guardian for a large
number of orphaned and troubled teenage boys. He lived in the
small mill town of Porterdale. His family owned the textile mill and
employed most everyone in town. His house was a large, twelve-room
mansion located on a hill, just on the outskirts of town. Margolin was
born in 1899, so he was in his fifties when he became a part of the
orphans' lives. He was very involved and charitable to the community.

Being president of the family mill and chairman of the local bank, Margolin was the most respected man in town. He was honored by then Governor Marvin Griffin for his unselfish efforts to provide troubled teens with the opportunity to learn a skill or trade and not end up on the path to prison. Margolin's rehabilitation plan was to bring these young men, always without families and most from long distances, to Porterdale for job training. He was constantly parading them around town, showing everyone how well they were being reformed. He claimed his successes came from placing the young men in jobs throughout the country, having them start over in new places with new horizons.

What was really going on . . . was human trafficking.

His income, it was later revealed, had not come from the textile mill. The mill was actually losing money. He made his living selling these young men to several copper mines in South America. From what we can tell, Margolin spent a few weeks in Peru in the fall of 1949. It was a business trip for the mill, and we can only assume that's when he made the deal. Records recovered from the mill show the boys were taught to operate and repair machinery. It appears they were not sold to operate shovels but to provide mechanical and technical services. He would send them out west to El Paso, Texas, where his partner, Charles Martin, would then move them to Guadalajara, Mexico, through Central America, to their final destination: Pucallpa, Peru.

Martin and Margolin did this for twelve years. It was said they trafficked over a thousand young men during this period. Margolin did send a small percentage to legitimate businesses in the states and every now and then brought them back to Porterdale to show off his "success." The only reason it stopped was that Charles Martin died of a sudden heart attack in 1962. Margolin no longer had a partner to continue that arm of the trade.

Margolin had a wife, three children, and four grandchildren, and no one ever knew what he was really up to. Believe it or not, Margolin was never caught or punished for his crime, at least not on this earthly plane. This all came to light after his death in 1973. His family was remodeling the house and found a hidden vault in the basement containing all the records and accounts.

There was a big push in 1975 to discover the fate of these young men, and the state of Georgia sent an investigative team to Peru. For some reason, the Peruvian government denied anything of the sort ever happened and would not allow the investigation team access to any of the copper mines' records. With no relatives coming forward and no one to prosecute, the whole issue faded away into the horrible abyss of human injustice.

That's the story Mark McClure came to film. It's a story long forgotten, and one he said needed to be documented.

The production crew was fortunate enough to be allowed access to the old mill and the Margolin estate. I guess the family was still carrying the guilt and wanted to wash clean the stain of their father's sins. I was moved by the story and returned to the set the following day, ready to play the role of Doris, Margolin's wife.

The people of Porterdale were gathered around the production site, excited to see all the activity. The set was located on the west side of the town's square, and crew members were preparing for a sunrise scene. Most of the downtown area was blocked off and had been cleared of any modern signage or cars. The director had procured about twenty cars from the 1950s from a local collector and strategically positioned them around the square. Fortunately for the set designers, the town had progressed very little since the 1960s. The fall of the textile industry had frozen the little town in time.

For the cast, the crew had staged and roped off a small area. Inside the ropes were chairs, refreshments, and general comforts to help us prepare for and endure a long day of filming. My character, Doris, would not be introduced until the end of the week. I found a seat and watched as the crew got ready for the first scene. I was lost in thought when I heard someone calling in my direction.

"Ma'am. . . . Excuse me, ma'am." I looked over to see a young couple trying to get my attention. They took a flash photo and excitedly motioned me over to the rope. I did not recognize them but walked over to see what they wanted.

"Thank you so much for coming over! Can we please have your autograph?" the young lady asked as she shoved a pen and pad my way. I must have immediately flushed. I could feel the heat coming to my cheeks, and I was speechless. I don't know what I expected, but it was not to be asked to sign an autograph. We both just stood there— me with a look of embarrassment and the couple with toothy grins. *What the hell*, I thought. *I'll scribble something illegible and they will never be the wiser.* I signed the pad and stood there for another picture.

"Thank you, Ms. Reese," the young girl said, holding close her "movie star's" autograph. I had no idea how she knew my name until I realized I was wearing an official cast ID that read "Aubrey Reese." I would love to be a fly on the wall when they Googled my name and found that I was not an actor but an artist who made tables out of old doors.

That Friday, after a week of filming downtown, the set moved to the Margolin estate, a few blocks south. One of the casting directors said I would not be needed until early next week but to be back on Monday morning. I had pretty much sat around all week doing nothing. This would have been very frustrating had I not received a payment of a thousand dollars. It wasn't just that I never appeared in a single scene; I counted about fifteen others who were paid for just standing around. What a waste of time and money. I stashed the hundred dollar bills in my shirt and let them worry about the budget.

—

By the time I'd filled Colby and Nathan in about the movie set, it was eleven a.m.

"I know I'm dragging it out," I said, "but I think you should hear all the details to understand everything that's happened. Both of you better double up on the coffee, because the story is about to take a bizarre twist."

We took a break and walked outside to stretch our legs. The dogs were on the front porch diligently looking up the road for trouble. Nathan and Colby took the opportunity to bring in more firewood, and I refreshed our coffee. Then we gathered on the couches and I continued my story.

I showed up the following Monday expecting a flurry of activity, but by then, things had changed. Mark was not around and had not been since the first day. I sensed a cold, withdrawn feeling from the crew, and there was no longer the exciting feel of a movie set. Around ten o'clock, the directors retreated to the production trailers and did not return until late afternoon. I asked several of the crew why things had stopped, but they just shrugged their shoulders.

As the week continued, things did not improve. By Friday, I quit inquiring and decided it was going to be my last day. With a thousand dollars in my pocket, it was time to head to Madison and put this strange mess behind me—and that's when he showed up. I was almost to my car when I caught a glimpse of him entering one of the production trailers. Looking back, I should have continued walking, but I didn't. I approached the trailer and knocked on the door.

"Come in," I heard Mark say. I opened the door and looked in. He was sitting at a desk, going through the contents of his briefcase. He abruptly closed it as I approached. "Hey," he said as he briefly stood and motioned me toward the desk. "Come on in. You've been on my mind, and I was hoping to catch you before you left."

"I was wondering when you would show up," I said, walking in and approaching the desk.

"It's been crazy the last week," Mark said, throwing his hands up in the air. "I've been to Los Angeles, San Francisco, New York, Portland, and, believe it or not, Des Moines, Iowa."

"Wow, that's a lot of traveling. Mind if I ask why the whirlwind tour?"

"Well, we're filming movies and documentaries, similar to the Margolin project, all over the country. I have project managers at each location, and I've been checking on the progress of the productions." Changing the subject, he asked, "How are things on set?"

"Not the way I expected," I replied. "We've done very little since filming the opening scenes. They changed the set location to the Margolin estate, and we've yet to film anything. It seems everything stopped after the first few days. I'm glad I got to see you, because today is my last day," I said, making my way toward the door.

Mark immediately jumped out of his seat and rushed over to block the door. "What—you can't leave!" he said, slightly exasperated. "Listen, I'm on the set now, and things will be different. It may seem like nothing is happening, but I promise they are. As a matter of fact, more than you would ever believe. Trust me when I tell you how important the next few weeks will be," Mark said, speaking fast and convincingly.

I didn't know what to say. He seemed overly dramatic and even slightly panicked. I didn't know how I could be that important to the movie. I figured one more week couldn't hurt, so I agreed.

As I was leaving, Mark said, "Next week may be the most important week of your life."

As monumental as that sounds, it was an understatement compared to what was to come.

—

Arriving at my Jeep, I was just about to open the door when someone firmly grabbed my arm. I spun around to see a young Asian girl. I recognized her from the set and quickly pulled my arm from her grasp.

"What the hell are you doing?" I yelled while backing up against the car.

"Please calm down, Ms. Reese. I just need to ask you a few questions," the girl replied, nervously looking around the parking lot.

"Questions about what?" I demanded to know.

"What were you and Mr. McClure discussing in the trailer?" she asked suspiciously.

"What? That's none of your business!" I said while aggressively moving away from the Jeep toward the girl. After my initial shock, I was beginning to regain my composure. "You better have a damn good reason for this, or you'll find yourself off the set and maybe in jail!" I added sternly while rubbing my arm.

Seeing that my shouting was starting to draw attention, the girl stepped closer and said, "You have no idea what you've gotten yourself involved in."

I just stood there, defiant. "*Gotten myself involved in*, what the hell does that mean?" I was becoming more irritated by the second. They obviously had me confused with someone else!

"Ms. Reese, my name is Mia Kwan, and I'm an agent with the Federal Bureau of Investigation. It would be in your best interest if you cooperated. Are you headed back to Madison?" she asked as she held out an official-looking badge with her picture and ID.

I looked at the badge and assumed it was real. I had never seen one before and could not believe I was now.

"Yes, I am going back to Madison, but I'm not sure I want to talk to you. What's this all about?" I asked.

"Meet me at Hill Park in thirty minutes, and I will explain everything. Do not make or receive any phone calls. Do not stop or communicate with anyone. Drive straight to Hill Park. This is very important; do I make myself clear?" the agent asked.

I could tell she was serious, and I knew I had little choice. "Yes, I'll be there in thirty minutes," I replied.

I drove the next half hour in a confused state. What kind of trouble could I possibly be involved in? To my knowledge, I had not witnessed any criminal activity and was just an extra in a cheap movie, for God's sake!

I pulled up to Hill Park and saw Agent Kwan and a man sitting at a table. I parked the car and approached them.

"Please sit down, Ms. Reese, and thank you for coming. As I said, I'm Agent Kwan, and this is Agent Holmes, Jonathan Holmes," Agent Kwan said, making the introduction.

With all that was happening, his name brought images to mind, and I could not help but feel a smile forming. I think he knew it was coming.

"Jonathan Holmes. Let me guess: Your friends call you John," I slyly said.

He sheepishly studied his black patent leather shoes and said, "Yes, ma'am, that's what they call me."

"That is quite a *big* name to live up to," I said with a smile.

Everyone seemed to share the awkward moment, and then Agent Kwan broke the silence. "Okay, time for a few questions."

"How long have you known Mr. McClure, and how close are you?" Agent Kwan asked.

"We're not close at all. I didn't know him until about two weeks ago and was only helping him find stage props for the set. I spent maybe two afternoons with him. He invited me to visit the set and maybe play a role in the movie. Of course I was skeptical but decided to check it out. I saw him on the first day of the production and had not seen him since until a few minutes before you tried to pull my arm off," I replied.

"Well, as you know, I've been on the set the entire time and have watched you very carefully. Although we had our suspicions, we don't believe you have anything to do with McClure and his group. I got a feeling you were fed up and were about to leave the production," Agent Kwan said, looking at me with a serious expression. "We need you to stay with the movie. No one has been able to get close to McClure, and you seem to have his attention. We need you to assist us with our investigation," she explained.

"None of this makes any sense. I'm an artist from Madison trying to make a few extra bucks in a movie; what help could I possibly be to the FBI?" I asked, totally bewildered.

"I know you're going to find this hard to believe, but you were not just singled out at the antique market in Decatur—McClure and his group have been researching and investigating you for the past month. We don't have a lot of info, but we've intercepted enough to know he wants to recruit you into his group. We are unable to come up with a reason. Would you have any idea why?" Agent Kwan asked.

Group? What group? My mind was running a mile a minute! How the hell could this be happening? How did she know about us meeting in Decatur? Was the FBI following me? I just wanted to drive the few short streets to my house and forget the whole day ever happened. "No, I have no idea what they could possibly want with me. I've never been part of a group in my life. What kind is it?" I asked.

"Well, before we go into details, you should know that McClure is planning something very serious," she said. "The plan, of which we have few details, has implications that could affect the entire country. The fact that McClure has singled you out and wants to recruit you is the break we've been looking for. I know this is all overwhelming, but we're running out of time, and at this point, we don't have enough evidence to warrant a search or an arrest. All we ask is for you to come to the Atlanta headquarters and listen to our proposition." Agent Kwan and Holmes waited on my reply.

Surreal is the only word I can come up with to describe that bizarre day. It was Friday afternoon, and my plans were to grab a pizza, swing by Ingles for a bottle of wine, and paint an old dresser until the pizza and wine were gone. Now it appeared I was headed to the FBI headquarters for God knows what.

"Can I go home first and change my clothes and freshen up?" I asked.

They both looked at each other, and I knew the answer.

"We really don't have time for that," Kwan said. "They are expecting us within the hour."

I was wondering if I even had a choice. I locked the doors to my Jeep and got in the big black Chevrolet Suburban. We left Madison driving west, and I noticed the fire-red sun setting over Atlanta. It appeared as if the city were on fire and we were driving straight into the inferno. I took this as an omen for things to come.

—

I took a break from the story and glanced at my rescuers. By then, we'd been in Warthen nearly twenty-four hours. Time for another break. I wasn't feeling much better but no longer wanted to take the Lortab. I'd had an adverse reaction in the past, causing me to act and carry on in an irresponsible and uncontrollable manner. I asked for some ibuprofen, but Colby had other thoughts. He cautioned that the severe pain could possibly come back and I should not stop taking the Lortab. He offered to monitor me for the rest of the day and throughout the night.

But that wasn't what I wanted. I walked over and sat on the couch.

Reluctantly, he retrieved the ibuprofen and joined us in the den.

"Okay, so now is where things really start to get interesting," I began.

And that's when Colby lost it.

"Interesting?" he asked sarcastically. "Well, it's about time! So far it's just been a normal, boring last two days. It's been weeks since I've blown up an RV and almost been killed by God knows who! Hell, I can barely remember the last time I've been shot at and had to escape for my life. Please continue. I can hardly wait for the interesting part."

"I mean the story, not what's happened to us," I yelled. Why don't you just shut up and try not to be such a smartass! You never could stand it if you weren't the center . . ."

"Stop it! Both of you," Nathan sternly said.

I gave Colby an icy stare and continued the story.

—

We got to the FBI headquarters, and they escorted me to an office that appeared to be about ten stories underground. Mia and John introduced me to their boss, and we all sat at a large conference table. There were a few others in the room, but I can't remember their names. I was exhausted at that point, on top of being anxious. Kwan's boss (I think her name was Hammonds) nodded toward her to start the meeting. She got straight to the point:

"Okay, here's what we know. McClure and his group are using the movie production company as a front and have strategically placed production sets all across the country. We've identified production sets similar to Porterdale in San Francisco, Los Angeles, Portland, Dallas, and several other states. He has geographically covered the entire country, with Atlanta seemingly his base. From what we can tell, a core group of about fifteen people meet in Atlanta at least once a month. They did meet quarterly, but over the past year, they have stepped it up to monthly. The résumés of these individuals are extraordinary. McClure himself is quite impressive.

"He was born in Decatur, Georgia, in 1962. His childhood seemed to be unremarkable other than the fact he was highly intelligent and excelled in school. He graduated from Towers High School at sixteen and was accepted at Georgia Tech just shy of his seventeenth birthday. In high school, he kept to himself and had very few, if any, friends.

"That all changed when he arrived at Georgia Tech. Tech had developed a specialized engineering program and searched the country for extremely intelligent kids. Their IQs had to be above 140, and their SAT scores had to be perfect or very close to perfect. McClure was the most promising of the group and had the highest scores. These kids quickly found each other, formed a strong bond, and separated themselves from the student population.

"McClure's major area of study was molecular science and biochemical engineering. He later became interested in genetics and earned his master's degree and doctorate in genetic engineering. His peers excelled in similar studies and had the degrees to match. Needless to say, we are talking about some of the brightest minds in the world. Creating their own little group, these young kids alienated themselves and failed to mesh with the student population. Georgia Tech only kept the program for a couple years, discontinuing it for unknown reasons. Post college, the group continued to meet.

"Through years of isolation from society, their bond grew stronger. McClure has been the group's leader from the start. He made his fortune in his late twenties by developing and patenting the process to create genetically modified food. He sold the patents to ConAgra in his early thirties and, until starting the movie production company, never worked again.

"Somewhere along the line, the group's philosophies, ideologies, and beliefs began to take shape. And as you can imagine, their views were empirical and counter societal. No one had any idea this group existed, but that all changed after September 11, 2001.

"After nine-eleven, the NSA and Homeland Security developed software that scanned emails, text messages, and phone conversations. Unknown to the public, the software was scanning all media for particular words and phrases with terroristic undertones. Known as the Homeland Security Presidential Directive 6 (HASPD-6), a multi-agency task force was created to identify and track individuals or groups that repeatedly used such language.

"In the spring of 2011, McClure and his group were added to the terrorist watch-list database. The FBI, being part of the multi-agency task force, was given the responsibility to track the activities of McClure and his group. Our investigation was proceeding well until June of 2012. McClure and his group suddenly dropped out of communication. We had figured that with the technical intelligence of McClure and his associates, it was just a matter of time before they realized they were being monitored.

"We speculate that McClure started the movie production business as a way to communicate and discuss the group's plans. This happened in January of 2012. Many of the individuals on the watch list are on site and directing the various movies and documentaries located across the country. As I said before, they all meet in Atlanta at least once a month at various locations.

"We've maintained our distance since 2012 and believe now is the time to infiltrate the group. It appears that something major is about to happen, and it's time to step up our surveillance," Agent Kwan explained.

The room was silent, and all eyes were focused on me. They were waiting on a response, and with resignation, I gave them what they were looking for. "So what exactly do you want from me?" I asked.

"As I told you, McClure sought you out for a reason. He obviously has a plan for you, and we know it's not for the movie. All we want you to do is return to the set on Monday and continue to act normally. Maintain your impatience and frustration about how the production is proceeding. If he really has plans for you, it will become evident soon," Agent Kwan replied.

Chapter Nine

Colby

I t was late in the afternoon and we decided to take another break. Nathan and I had many questions that led to lengthy discussions. Aubrey was doing her best with such a detail-obsessed audience. Needing some fresh air and time to absorb it all, we pulled on our heavy coats and went for a walk. The cold grabbed us immediately, and the wind snatched Aubrey's hat and tossed it away. I retrieved it and pulled it over her head in an exaggerated and playful manner. She laughed and caught me in the ribs with a mean punch. Damn if the memories did not come back. I could see Nathan smiling and knew what he was thinking.

We headed in the direction of the pond with Hannah and Savannah on point. I kept a watchful eye on the surrounding woods. Before we left, I'd retrieved my Colt 1911 .45 and handed Nathan a loaded Glock Model 19 .40—there was no discussion why.

We stopped at the dock and tried to enjoy the peaceful nature of the surroundings. The wind was creating small whitecaps on the water, and the longleaf pines slowly swayed, moving in a hypnotic rhythm. A skein of geese appeared in a V, making a low approach toward the pond. Seeing us at the last minute, they pulled up, honking their displeasure. We watched as they performed aerobatic maneuvers, veering hard right and straight up and then flying across the adjacent hill. For a brief time, we were lost from our troubles. It was hard to believe that at that exact moment there were people desperately wanting to find and kill us.

Evening was looming as shadows appeared on the landscape. Walking back to the house, I felt a creeping sense of nervousness, wondering if the pursuers might be lying in wait. I instructed Aubrey and Nathan (as well as Hannah and Savannah) to advance from the front while I approached from the rear. All appearing clear, we entered the house to a warm and welcoming fire. I noticed Aubrey massaging her head and generously offered to get her a Lortab. We all got a needed laugh, and I headed to the kitchen to start supper.

Nathan cleared a spot on the table in front of the fire. It was actually a coffee table Aubrey had made from an old door. I think my collection was up to four. Bourguignon stew (previously prepared and from the freezer) was the soup du jour, accompanied by a French baguette and a bottle of Bordeaux from Chateau Moulin de Beausejour. We sat Indian style by the fire and enjoyed supper, laughing and telling stories from Madison. Nathan and Aubrey became better acquainted since thus far our only conversations had been concerning our dire situation. They had much in common, and I think Aubrey changed her "creep-from-wine-club" opinion.

After eating supper and finishing the bottle of wine, we fell into a sense of melancholy, knowing we again had to face our circumstances. Nathan suggested we rotate a watch throughout the night. I assured him that if anything happened within two hundred yards of the house, Hannah and Savannah would immediately alert us. We retired to our bedrooms hoping the night would be uneventful, peaceful, and quiet.

—

After a restless night, imagining every noise was an invading force of killers, I finally gave up on the idea of sleep around six a.m. It appeared my partners had no issues as Aubrey was still in her room and I could hear Nathan snoring on the other side of the house.

Entering our third day on the run, I had to believe McClure and his group had not forgotten us. From Aubrey's overview and from what I'd witnessed, I knew our future still hung precariously in the balance. It was time for some action, and what I needed to accomplish was better done alone.

I fixed coffee for "Beauty and the Beast" and headed out into the woods.

As previously mentioned, I had brought south my knowledge and special supplies from my days in the Great North and had relocated them in strategic areas on my farm. My thoughts at the time were on possibly protecting my property from roving bands of desperate people after an EMP strike or an economic collapse, not from a terrorist version of *Revenge of the Nerds*.

Nonetheless, I was prepared, come what may, and it was time to put the plan into action.

My first line of defense (other than a well-designed and coordinated plan) was a protected perimeter. Through aerial and topographic maps, I had developed a grid of my two hundred acres. I'd identified the most accessible points and designed natural blockades in the narrowest and lowest areas. With short notice, I could have these blockades in place.

Next, I'd set up internal lines of defense at varying intervals from the perimeter of the houses. The closer to the houses, the more concentrated the intervals. I'd had to decide between two different strategies of engagement. One strategy was posting that the property was monitored, armed, and protected. This would ward off all but the most aggressive and well-prepared attackers. The other strategy was a clandestine approach. I chose the latter.

High in the trees, camouflaged and concealed, I'd positioned AirSight 1080p infrared, wireless IP video cameras. Mounted on swivel brackets, they could rotate 360 degrees. The cameras were covered from the weather and configured with weatherproof Thomson wireless routers placed at intervals to connect the whole system. A redundancy system was also installed in case the primary system was detected. In areas of lowest access or priority, I placed listening devices in lieu of cameras. These devices were made by Ericksen Electronics and incorporated with a digital software program that filtered out animal and consistent ambient noises (airplanes, streams, rain, etc.).

In the closet of the main bedroom in the main house was a hatch that led to a tunnel. (Okay, maybe at this point I've started to qualify as paranoid prepper!) After about ten feet, the tunnel split in two directions. One led to the storage room of the May House, a restored house from the 1830s. In the attic of the May House, behind a concealed door, I'd installed an electronic monitoring station that linked the entire system. In the other direction, the tunnel stretched about fifty yards and led to an old doghouse just inside the woods. The doghouse sat on a hinged foundation that covered the exit.

In the event of a crisis, this system would be an aid to sentries posted along the perimeter and interior sections of the property. My plan included a group of trained individuals (Red River Valley boys) who would immediately relocate to Warthen and domicile until the crisis was over. It might be a long way from Stony Mountain, but this group monitored the media and would know the shit was about to hit the fan well in advance of the rest of the population. Most of them were loners with no family and had pledged that they would head straight to Warthen to help me defend my life and property. I think they would have done it more for the adventure of the trip than their allegiance toward me.

In a situation like I was currently embroiled in, the system would act more as an early warning system, allowing for escape. I did have a stash of weapons and other interesting items with which I could hold off a small attack for a limited time by myself.

I jumped on an ATV and made my rounds through the property. All the cameras and electronic devices looked solid and appeared to be working correctly. I checked and tested the monitoring panel in the attic of the May House and inspected the backup generator. With everything thoroughly surveyed, I headed back to the main house.

Aubrey and Nathan were in the den, having coffee and bagels. I joined them and explained that the dogs and I had gone for a little walk. I decided to keep my activities to myself.

Aubrey continued her story.

CHAPTER TEN

Aubrey

On Monday, with a sense of dread, I returned to the set. The filming locations were the Margolin estate and the mill. The house was stately and beautifully situated on a hill overlooking the Yellow River. It was juxtaposed with the meager mill houses surrounding it. The house was in view of the mill, and I wondered what the workers must have thought looking out the windows as they worked twelve-hour days at their looms.

Arriving early, I found a coffee shop downtown and sat contemplating my situation. I had not pondered long before I saw Mark drive up in his black Audi R8 and disappear behind the gate to the mill lofts and office complex. Downtown Porterdale had changed very little in the past few decades, but the mill area had been transformed into a chic bedroom community. The lofts were reminiscent of the retail areas in the old Decatur Mill District.

Within a few minutes, Mark appeared in the coffee shop and immediately noticed me sitting in the corner. He made a beeline towards me. Nervous and apprehensive, I could feel the moisture on my hands and willed against a handshake.

"Good morning," Mark said as he approached.

"Good morning, and good to see you actually came to work!" I said in jest.

"Well, I'm a man of my word, and I told you I would be here. After our talk on Friday, I was wondering if you would show up," he replied.

I invited him to sit and knew it was time to find out where all this was going. His comment was a great opportunity to question him and gauge his reaction. My question was an honest one, so it required no acting. "After our conversation on Friday, I couldn't help but wonder why you think I'm so important to this production. I have no acting experience, and my role in the film is just an extra. Of course, I was flattered with Friday's plea to keep me involved, but I'm not sure I understand it."

I could see his discomfort and knew I'd caught him off guard.

"Well, that's a valid question, and quite frankly, there is something else I would like to talk to you about," he said.

No longer feeling as nervous, I just sat there with a neutral expression. I was not going to blink first and waited for him to continue.

"My intentions were not to leave you on the set for two weeks without seeing you," he said. "As I said on Friday, I've been very busy traveling, and my schedule's been intense. Why don't we meet for lunch and I will explain everything?" he suggested.

"Sounds fine. Let's meet upstairs at Jimbo's Grill. As you just stated, I've spent the last two weeks in Porterdale and have found a favorite lunch spot," I said with confidence.

"Great. See you at noon," Mark replied as he gathered his briefcase and headed for the door.

I left the coffee shop just after Mark and drove the short distance to the set. The production crew was setting up at the mill, and there was a flurry of activity. Mark had apparently gotten the word out that the crew needed to have more of a presence; I wondered if he was doing this for me. Either way, I was almost drawn back into the excitement of the documentary. All the actors were on the set, and there were more extras than in the previous weeks. About a hundred spectators had turned up to watch the filming and were lined up along the edge of the production zone. I found my chair in the roped-off area designated for the actors and crew, and I spent most of the morning watching as well. As noon approached, I became more nervous about the upcoming meeting with Mark.

When the time arrived, I entered Jimbo's and climbed the stairs to the second floor. Mark and another man were sitting at an outside table, deep in conversation. I felt things were about to take a direction from which I could not return. Taking a deep breath and running through a quick prayer, I approached them.

Possessing information I was not supposed to have was a dual-edged sword. On one hand, I had the distinct advantage of being prepared for the discussion I anticipated. On the other, I had to be careful not to divulge what I knew and to display the proper emotions and reactions. I reminded myself of this as the two men stood to greet me.

"Aubrey, good to see you. Glad you could join us," Mark said uncomfortably with a fake smile. I don't think he knew whether to shake my hand, give me a hug, or do nothing.

"Glad to be here," I replied. Mark glanced at the man standing next to him and made the introduction. "Jason Keel, meet Aubrey Reese."

We shook hands and exchanged pleasantries. As soon as we sat, the waitress appeared and took our order. We made small talk about Jason and Mark attending Georgia Tech together and my growing up in a small town. After about ten minutes, the waitress returned with our lunch. We hurried through our meal, anticipating the conversation that was to follow.

"Aubrey, I hope you don't mind, but I was telling Jason a little bit about you and your situation. It has to be a challenge, living in such a small apartment and barely making ends meet. I'm sure at times it would be so easy to move back to Jewell and build your furniture there," Mark said, attempting to sound matter-of-fact. This, of course, was a test. He knew perfectly well I had not given him that information, and it was time for me to put on a show.

"Wait . . . What are you talking about? I never told you any of that. How do you know where I live?" I demanded to know.

Neither said a word. They both just sat, staring at me.

"Who in the hell do you think you are, prying into my private life? I don't know what your motives are, but you have stepped way out of bounds," I said as I threw back my chair and headed for the stairs.

I was just about to reach my car when Mark rushed up behind me. "Look, Aubrey, please let me explain. Please give me five minutes. If you don't want to hear any more, you are free to leave."

"Free to leave?" I exclaimed. "You don't tell me when I am free to do anything," I yelled. "You have five minutes, only because I want to hear what possibly could have warranted this poking around in my personal life. What the hell was that all about?" I asked furiously as I pointed up to the restaurant.

"I did not plan on having this conversation in a parking lot, but I guess my actions leave me no choice. So, here goes. I did not just happen to be at the Decatur Antique Market—I followed you there.

I never had any intention of you playing a part in the documentary; it was just a reason to guarantee that I would see you again. No, I am not a stalker obsessed with you . . . I have more important reasons," Mark said.

I did not have to act shocked at what he was telling me; I truly was. Of course, I knew McClure was planning something sinister, but it had just sunk in that I could possibly end up as a central figure. Things were becoming more bizarre by the minute.

"Continue," I said, becoming a little calmer.

I could see his expression of partial relief as I allowed him to further explain. "We were setting up the Margolin documentary and needed a few more antique props. Someone mentioned Madison as a good spot to find them. As I pulled into Madison on 441 North, I noticed a big sign advertising antiques. That was when I made my fateful stop that brings us here today. I walked in, and you were the first person I saw. You immediately caught my attention and held it. I would like to say it was your physical attractiveness, but it was more than that. As much as I am a man of science and focused solely in that endeavor, I found myself confused by pure emotion. I could not explain it, and generally I can explain everything.

"Later, as I made my way to the counter, I witnessed you in a confrontation with a customer who was upset about the amount of sales tax. It had recently increased, and she was complaining about it. You said that with the current administration, the extra one percent should be the least of her worries. You were not being sarcastic, just making light of the situation. But she became belligerent and told you that you should respect the president and his policies. She stated that this country and the world were changing and that the wealthy would no longer hold the working man hostage. It was time for everyone to get their share and what they deserved.

"Her main point was unequivocally that the rich were no longer in charge and that the president would see their wealth spread out to the people. I was not surprised by her speech or demeanor. I travel this entire country and see that attitude wherever I go. It is a growing philosophical, idealistic cancer. Intelligent, individual thought is becoming a rare commodity. The degradation of the individual accomplishment is more prevalent than ever. Apathy and entitlement seem to be the direction of the nation. It is obvious at both ends of the economic spectrum.

"But, back to why I later followed you to the Decatur Antique Market. After the woman left, I could see you were about to comment on what had just happened to a woman working with you behind the counter. I eased a little closer to hear your response. You said much of what I just said, but one comment caught my attention. I was shocked to hear you say it. I'm not sure I have ever heard a layperson make the connection. It is the concept on which I've based my entire research and focus, the same concept on which some of the world's greatest minds are currently concentrating. I'm sure you asked the question in its rhetorical form, because I could see that you understood the truth of what you were saying. Do you remember the question you asked your co-worker?"

My mind searched back to the day and conversation Mark was referencing. It only took a second to recall the confrontational customer, and I easily remembered my question. I also remembered the blank stare I received from the clerk after asking it. It was obviously not a mainstream thought, and I was mostly venting my frustration and was not expecting an answer. My studies at Georgia College and State University had been in behavioral science and social anthropology. We'd regularly discussed theories on the evolution of biological thought processes and how the changes could affect society. I had not thought about these things in years, but the attitude of the customer brought it all back.

"Yes, I remember the question," I answered. *"Is it possible that the direction of intellectual thought on a universal scale could effect an evolutionary change? Could the greed of some, mixed with the ineptness of others, actually change the course and direction of mankind?"*

Mark looked at me with a serious, solemn expression and said, "I knew right then that you were one of us and fate had brought us together."

As strange as it sounds, at that moment I did feel an odd form of acceptance. I had, in fact, asked that question and did wonder if there was a correlation. I watched Mark's expression as he took note of my reaction. He knew he had made a connection. He also knew at that point he would ask me to be a part of his group and part of his plan. The expression on his face was one of admiration. What he failed to know was that one day he would only feel betrayal when he looked at me. He asked me to return to the set on Tuesday and said he would go into further detail.

I just smiled and said, "See you in the morning."

Mark then left me to rejoin Jason.

With an ominous feeling of doom, I drove away from Jimbo's and Porterdale. I needed to get downtown and report all that had happened to Kwan and Holmes. Since my role in the documentary, which it was now apparent I would probably never play, was not scheduled until later in the week, I took off the rest of the afternoon.

Driving back to Atlanta, I exited I-20 onto Spring Street. Looking west, I could see the approaching darkness as gray clouds began overtaking the blue sky. I thought about the intersecting of lives in such a short time span. Two weeks before, I had known none of these people, and now I was racing back to Atlanta to report to the FBI about a suspected terrorist group of which I might soon be a member. Not that I was excited or thrilled about being in that position, but it was interesting to think that, in the great cosmic scheme of life, a chance meeting had led to that exact moment. In the course of a two-minute random conversation in earshot of a stranger, I had gone from being a clerk at a small-town antique market to playing a major role in a potential good-versus-evil confrontation. I had no idea where the adventure was headed; I was just along for the ride.

Kwan and Holmes had given me the address of a local Whole Foods store, and we were to meet in the southeast corner of the parking lot. I had no idea where the hell the southeast corner was located and just parked on the side and to the left. As a precautionary measure, my instructions were to go inside and shop for about five minutes and then return to my Jeep. After a few minutes of mindless shopping, I returned to my Jeep to find two anxious agents waiting for me. They nervously scanned the influx of incoming cars and instructed me to follow them to my new temporary apartment—very temporary, as I would soon find out.

We drove for a few miles and ended up somewhere in the vicinity of Ponce de Leon Avenue. They led me into a very nice two-bedroom apartment with views of the city. If I had to spend time away from home, this would not be a bad spot, I thought.

We spent the next hour or so discussing my conversation with McClure and Jason Keel. They seemed pleased with the information and the direction of the case. The hour was early, but I was worn out. All this double-agent business had taken its toll. Anticipating the flurry of activity to come, I wanted a good night's rest and ushered Kwan and Holmes to the door.

Before leaving, Kwan paused and said, "Ahh... Aubrey, tonight will be your only night in this apartment. Tomorrow you will be moving into the RV."

"What RV?" I asked.

She hesitated, looking back at Holmes. "Well... anticipating that McClure will invite and accept you into the group, the bureau's analyst decided to place you in an RV not far from the set. He feels the RV is an indication of a nomadic independence, and that's what we need McClure to see. He has to believe you are disconnected from society and he has to have no fear that you might back out or are not be trusted. We've parked it on Wheat Street in Porterdale."

I didn't mind the idea of an RV and told her it was fine.

She again hesitated and seemed uncomfortable. "There are a couple of things you need to know. Uh... it's not the greatest of RVs, and... umm... you will not be alone..."

Both agents were looking at the floor, and I knew this was not going to be good. "What do you mean, I won't be alone?" I asked, knowing I would probably not like her answer.

"Well... again, the analyst thought you needed to be portrayed as an eccentric and has placed a few cats in the RV. He feels the cats will be a symbol of your disillusionment with people and society," Kwan said with a conviction that seemed contrived.

I immediately shouted my objections. "That's not going to happen! I don't mind the RV so much, but I have to draw the line on the cats! I hate cats, and there's no way in hell I'm sleeping in an RV with a bunch of nasty cats," I loudly protested.

Holmes shrugged his shoulders and quickly slipped out the door. Kwan cautiously walked forward and handed me a slip of paper.

"Aubrey, this is the address where the RV is parked. Grab a few things from your apartment and plan to stay there until this thing is over. Hopefully it will be soon," Kwan said as she backed toward the door. "I am really sorry about this and promise to do my best to make it up to you."

After they left, I realized this would be my last evening in a comfortable bed and without the smell of cat piss. I moved to the kitchen to prepare supper from the few items I'd purchased at Whole Foods. It was not much—brie, crackers, and some tarragon chicken salad. I did notice that someone from the FBI had been gracious enough to leave a bottle of wine, and I thought it was considerate until I went to open it and noticed the name—La Chateau Le Chat, *The House of the Cat.*

—

As I left for Porterdale the next day, dark storm clouds hovered close to the horizon and were moving in fast from the west. Not only were storms predicted for the day, but Jim Morrison was on the radio, also warning me of riding an impending dangerous storm. If I had any damn sense, I would have forgotten this whole mess, for which I was horribly unprepared, and driven straight home to Madison. But, knowing I was committed, I exited I-20 East onto the Covington/ Oxford exit. Within a few short miles, I was entering Porterdale and in search of the RV.

I pulled to the end of Wheat Street, and there sat the bitch. I had pictured it in my mind, but I was sorely disappointed. It appeared to be from the 1970s and was a piece of junk! The hubcaps were missing, and it obviously had not been washed in years. Under the unfurled, mold-covered awning were a few cheap plastic chairs and a worn-out charcoal grill with only three legs. To my astonishment, there was a large TV antenna on the back side of the RV. It looked like it was from the sixties and belonged on a ranch-style house or a double-wide trailer. I walked up to the door and knew things were not going to get any better. As I peeked in, not quite having the courage to enter, I could not believe what I saw.

There they were, all lined up on the sleeper sofa and splayed out on the kitchen counter. They were all licking themselves in a disgusting way and stopped when I looked in. They were watching as if they had expected me. I left the door open, hoping they would make a dash for freedom, but none of them moved an inch.

Damn it! I noticed a litter box in the corner that was the size of a coffee table. It was already filling up with little brown crust-covered objects. Damn it again!

My first order of business was to spray the bottles of Lysol located on the counter and disinfect the RV. I sprayed the Lysol in the direction of the cats and they hit the floor, running toward the door, leaving me to survey my deplorable accommodations. It was worse on the inside than it was on the outside. The couch and chairs were made of cheap cloth and vinyl. They were horribly stained, and I could only imagine the events that had resulted in the stains.

There was a kitchenette with a stainless steel sink and cabinets made of plastic-covered faux wood. I opened the valve to the faucet, and a spit of brown water belched out. It smelled as bad as it looked. Next to the sink was the refrigerator, and I had no illusions it would be any better. It was not. With no power, it smelled of mold and mildew and only contained a few empty Milwaukee's Best beer cans. I think the FBI must have literally bought this piece of shit, with the cats included, from some miserable son of a bitch at a nearby trailer park. If they paid one hundred dollars, they had paid too much.

My feet stuck to the carpet as I made my way to the back bedroom. The mattress was stripped, and the result was a sight that I will not even begin to describe. I could start to feel that pasty feeling in my mouth that you get when you're seconds from throwing up. Thankfully, I had a bottle of water in the pocket of my jacket and took a few sips, which made me temporarily feel better. There were several packs of new sheets lying on the bed and, after soaking the mattress with Lysol, I made the bed.

Needing power, I walked outside and around to the back of the RV and found the electric hook up connector. I plugged it in with little expectation. It worked, and at least I had lights. There was propane for heat, and I got that going as well. I still could not believe I would have to spend even one night in this rolling feline hell. It was time to leave for the set, and it was going to be a long day with me knowing I had to return to this nightmare.

After a short drive, I arrived at the Margolin estate and signed in like every other morning. My MO was to just stand around, and I was getting pretty good at it. Doris, my character, was scheduled to have a minor role in a scene that day, but acting was the furthest thing from my mind—acting in the documentary, I should say.

It was not long before Mark showed up and pulled me over to one of the production trailers. As we walked inside, I noticed he was carrying a large shopping bag from Neiman Marcus. He sat the bag down on the desk and asked, "Do you have any plans for this evening?"

I gave him the proper response: "None that I cannot change."

He seemed pleased with my answer and said in a formal tone, "Great. I'm hosting a dinner party in Atlanta and request your company." He caught me looking at the Neiman Marcus bag. "I took the liberty to purchase you a few items. I know you're not settled right now and might not have access to your evening wear. Size four on the dress and seven and a half on the shoes, correct?"

"That's correct," I said, looking in the bag. There was a black, low-cut sequined dress with a pair of open-toed heels. There was also a small open box with a silver, multi-layered necklace and matching bracelet.

"Mark, this is all very beautiful. I don't know quite what to say." I really did not know what to say. Even if it was from a nutcase, I had never been given such exquisite gifts.

"Well, tonight is going to be a very important night. You're going to meet a group of my friends, and we will explain in detail what's happening. Here are the directions to the party," he said, handing me a printed card.

I left with the bags and loaded them into my Jeep. I returned to the set to discover that Doris's part would be delayed for yet another day. I was excused for the afternoon and could now concentrate on the evening's event. I wondered if Mark had had anything to do with the reschedule.

Pulling back up to the godforsaken RV, I dreaded taking the new, beautiful clothes inside. They would be immediately covered by the stench of cat. As I entered, they were purring or whatever you call the noise those nasty creatures make. I thought they wanted to be fed, so I threw some cat food in a dish and put it outside in hopes they would leave. Of course, they did not move. I held my breath until I got to the back bedroom and closed the door. It was not as bad back there, but still not pleasant. I had a few hours before heading to Atlanta and took a much-needed nap.

The directions were to an address on Paces Ferry Road in Buckhead—a very upscale, old-money, ostentatious community bordering Atlanta. Image is so important in Buckhead that even the housekeepers drive Mercedes. Parties are planned with an agenda. The host of the party, in most cases, is seeking a sizeable political or charitable donation. If you have been invited to a party, it's an unwritten rule to have your checkbook with you. The liquor will not stop flowing until a check is written. Of course, I knew I would not be writing a check—my stakes would be much higher.

I arrived to find two large iron gates with a guardhouse located between them. The invite did not mention if it were a private residence or a country club, but the entrance was quite impressive. Across the street and a few blocks down Paces Ferry was the Governor's Mansion. I was definitely out of my element and wondering what was going to be required of me.

Occupying the gatehouse were two well-armed, uniformed guards. As I pulled up, one of the guards approached my Jeep.

"Good evening, Ms. Reese," he said. Maybe I should have been surprised he knew my name, but I was not.

"Good evening," I said.

"Do you have the direction card that Mr. McClure gave you?" he politely asked.

"I do," I answered and handed him the card.

He scanned it with a small device and, after a confirming beep, said, "Thank you, Ms. Reese. If you will follow the drive, someone will greet you at the house."

"Thank you," I replied and pulled down the drive bordering the fine, manicured lawn. When I came upon the house, I could not believe the size. It was an elegant English Tudor with at least thirty rooms. It was larger and more magnificent than any of the homes on Paces Ferry Road—including the governor's. An attendant, also uniformed and armed, motioned for me to park in a line with several other cars. There was a Rolls Royce, Bentley, Mercedes Maybach, and my new favorite car I could never afford, a Porsche Panamera.

If this was in fact a house, whoever owned it would have to be in the upper half of the one percent. I was escorted to the front entrance and presented to another attendant. As soon as the door opened, I heard someone playing a piano and could feel the energy of the capacious room. Entering the foyer, I could see about twenty people mingling and socializing. Everyone was exquisitely dressed, and I felt good in my little black dress.

I had not been standing there long when a man approached and asked if I would like to try Mr. McClure's cabernet from his private vineyard. I guessed he was a sommelier, because he was wearing one of those silver tasting cups around his neck. He said the grape was from the 1992 production and had won numerous awards. Of course, I tried the wine, and, of course, it was fantastic. I don't think it would have ever touched the curves of Mark's crystal glass had it been any less impressive. Momentarily forgetting why I was there, I found myself reveling in the evening and thinking how exciting it was to be at such a grand affair, but those thoughts faded fast when I saw Mark approaching.

"Aubrey, how are you this evening? You look lovely," he said with a smile and relaxed tone. He was dressed in formal evening wear with matching ruby and diamond shirt studs and cuff links. He was charming and impressive.

"I'm doing fine, and thanks again for the dress and jewelry. Quite a dinner party," I replied honestly.

"Thank you. I'm just about to announce that dinner is being served." As Mark replied, a uniformed attendant appeared and lightly chimed a crystal bell to gain everyone's attention.

"Welcome to my home," Mark began. "Members of our group have traveled a great distance to be here tonight, figuratively and literally. Events are currently taking place that will begin the culmination of our twenty years of dedication and determination. As for tonight, enjoy the perks of the evening and each other's company. Over the next couple of days, we will meet and discuss the implementation of our long-awaited plan. Please find your place at the table," Mark instructed.

We were ushered into a dining hall that was reminiscent of its massive counterpart at the Biltmore Estate in Asheville, North Carolina. Mark stood at the head of the table waiting for everyone to take their seats. I noticed Jason Keel standing at the opposite end. I found my name card and sat down. There was no blessing of the meal, nor did I expect there to be. I enjoyed polite conversation with a gentleman seated to my left. He asked the usual questions and mentioned he handled the movie production's southwest division. He lived in Dallas, Texas, but was originally from Atlanta. He and Mark had attended Georgia Tech together. I had the feeling that most of the people in the room were former classmates from Tech.

After dinner and dessert, everyone migrated into the parlor near the front entrance. After the appropriate "mingle before departure," everyone began to leave. I was preparing to do the same when Mark appeared.

"Hey—do you mind staying a little longer? There are a few more people I want you to meet," he said. For one brief moment, I thought I might be able to slip out unnoticed, but it was time to face the inevitable.

"No, of course not. I'll be admiring your art collection while you say your goodbyes," I replied.

About ten minutes later, Mark found me studying a painting by Marc Chagall. I started to ask if it was an original, but I was sure it was.

"That is a painting he did in 1964, shortly after he created it on the ceiling of the Opera National de Paris Garnier," Mark stated.

"Beautiful," I replied.

"Come with me, and I will introduce you to my friends," Mark said as he motioned for me to join him in a nearby room. We entered the room, and I saw three people sitting around a table covered with papers. I noticed a fourth person with their back turned on the other side of the room.

"Aubrey, these four people are the inner circle of the organization I will be explaining to you. You might say we're the architects of the plan that has involved everyone present this evening. You know Jason Keel; you met him in Porterdale. The gentlemen to his left is Francis Young, and next to him is Thomas Hill," Mark said. "And of course," he said as the person on the other side of the room turned toward me, "you are acquainted with Ms. Kwan from the Margolin set."

Chapter Eleven

Mia Kwan walked toward us wearing the slightest of smiles. She stood next to Mark and said, "Hi, Aubrey. Sorry for all the confusion; we just have to be very careful."

Shocked would be an understatement to describe what I was feeling. I was speechless. I had the image of Kwan the FBI agent stuck in my brain. But here she was being introduced as one of the architects of the plan.

Mark suggested we join the others at the table. "Aubrey, I'm going to explain everything," he said. "I guess I should start with how Mia fits into all of this. Her father was a professor of molecular biology at Georgia Tech. He was our teacher, mentor, and friend. He took a group of us as very young students, and taught us science and how it applies—or should apply—to nature. Dr. Gming Lee is the reason we are here this evening. I wish Dr. Lee could be with us, but suffering from a mild stroke, he is unable to travel.

"Mia was adopted by the Lees from Korea just after her first birthday. Her biological parents were Mrs. Lee's brother and sister-in-law. They were killed in a tragic bus accident, leaving no one to care for Mia. Honoring her brother and sister-in-law, Mrs. Lee had Mia keep the surname Kwan," Mark explained.

"Dr. and Mrs. Lee raised Mia under the beliefs of our group, and she has been educated with our ideologies since her early youth. Unfortunately, Mrs. Lee passed away many years ago and never got the opportunity to see Mia excel and become an integral part of our group. Mia received her bachelor's degree in chemistry at the University of California at Santa Barbara. She also received, from the University of Virginia, a master's degree in psychology. She excelled as a student and completed her degrees in about half the time it would have taken most students. As you can imagine, she would have simply had to apply to the FBI and the job would have been hers. Actually, they recruited *her* while she was studying at Virginia.

"Neither Dr. Lee nor any of us connected with Mia was of interest back then to any of the national security agencies. Mia passed all the background checks with no problems and became an agent with the FBI.

"Because of the enormity and duration of what we were planning—something I will soon explain—we knew our work would eventually come to the attention of the government. When nine-eleven happened, it was inevitable. Mia finished her studies and joined the FBI in 2003, and it was not long before she took on a leadership role. In only three years, she became the lead agent of the counter-terrorism unit in Atlanta. This became very useful to our group as things began to take shape. It took many years to develop our plan, and just a few people knew about it, including Mia. As we approached the completion of our creation, it was time to unveil the plan to the entire group and set things in motion. Mia has been instrumental in deflecting any interest the FBI has had in our group. She is now the agent in charge of keeping an eye on us, and so far has kept the situation under her control. They know very little about what we are planning, thanks to her," Mark said as he smiled and looked at Mia.

I was trying to listen and comprehend what Mark was saying but could not wrap my mind around all the information about Mia. Was she really involved and committed to the group? Was her work with the FBI just a front? Did Mark know about my contact with her off the set? Was she waiting to tell Mark and the group about me tonight? She just stood there watching me while Mark spoke. I was trying not to show it, but I could feel the heat of panic and anxiety rush over me. I tried to focus on my breathing and not look at her.

"At this point, the FBI and Homeland Security have their hands full with real and potential terrorist threats, and we're listed as low priority. All the members in our group are law-abiding, taxpaying citizens. Most are at the top of their fields and well respected.

"We have waited twenty years for things to change and prove us wrong. It is apparent now that they will never change. I shall explain," Mark said.

"Evolution at its core is a paradox. It is a brutal, unforgiving, harsh order that is integrated into the delicate, harmonious rhythm of life. Its linear, dynamic process was set in motion at the beginning of time and shall always be.

"The process unfolded as it should have—until the onset of human intelligence. What seems to be the crown jewel of the evolutionary process may be the very thing that destroys it or at least sets it on an unintended course. In our arrogance, we believe we are supreme, but in the evolutionary process, we are only as significant as the smallest amoeba.

"As a group, we accept the fact that there is no set criterion or scientific formula for the directional growth of human intelligence. We've had countless debates about whether mankind's evolution is natural or manipulated. Admittedly, it is a philosophical question as much as a scientific one.

"At this point, man can continue his destructive path to eventual extinction, or some of us can intervene and save the human species. As Dr. Lee taught us so many years ago, the intelligent mind is evolution's gift to six million years of directional determination. To see it so dramatically corrupted with the irresponsible consumption of life-sustaining resources is not acceptable. The narcissistic mindset of today's society is the very thing that will destroy it.

"We cut and deplete the rainforest with very little regard to the rising carbon dioxide levels. We pollute our oceans and rivers daily with millions of tons of garbage, chemical toxins, and human waste with indifference toward the life-sustaining water. Global atmospheric and meteorological conditions are becoming more fragile by the year.

"Our kids are dying from cancers caused from toys created with toxic chemicals. Diseases are evolving and mutating faster than we can even classify them. Our antibiotics are becoming ineffective against the rapidly changing bacteria. There are strains of E. coli that, if they escaped quarantine, would be uncontrollable.

"We as biologists, scientists, and physicians see this every day. Our group has passively watched this worldwide demise and degradation of our biological and natural resources for far too long. No one has done anything of significance to address these dire issues. The World Health Organization is too mired in politics and is no longer effective. Does the general public have a sense of urgency concerning the destruction of our life resources or a future pandemic? No! People are too concerned about the latest version of the iPhone or the next generation of HD televisions.

"Nuclear proliferation by third world countries is imminent if not already a reality. Over the past two hundred years, this earth has seen more artificial and unnatural destruction by man, and, if left unchecked, he will destroy his home and himself. The recent disaster at the Fukushima nuclear plant in Japan is just one example. Accidents like Fukushima or Chernobyl will be more commonplace and will begin to occur worldwide.

"Over the years, our group has had many discussions on this catastrophic course of artificial evolutionary change. We realized from our early years at Tech that there would be dangerous consequences if this was left unchecked. We began as just ideological visionaries, frustrated with man's adulteration of the earth. We were extremely bright kids with no course or direction. Thankfully, Dr. Lee encouraged us to continue meeting after graduation and to use our gifts of intelligence to create change.

"The first four or five years after college, we were all building our careers and only met every few months. Our tight bond formed in college would continue to grow, with most of us planning our vacations together. It was fate that the majority of us would work and live in or around the Atlanta area. When we met, our central theme was always man's destructive course and how the problems were exponentially increasing worldwide. Our discussions led to great observations on man versus nature and how human intelligence seemed to be corrupting the balance, but our talks never led us in any particular direction. We were much like a ship without a rudder.

"Again, it was Dr. Lee who set us back on course. He had retired from Tech and begun to show more interest in our meetings. When he first joined us, we did not specifically have a cause, but that was soon to change. He increased our meetings to two a month.

"Over the course of a year, Dr. Lee began to lay out a bold plan of action. Admittedly, it was shocking at first, but we all knew in our hearts that in order to return to the delicate, balanced rhythm of creation, we must act decisively and directly.

"I was one of the few in our group who'd never married or reproduced. I had seen early on that I had no desire to bring a child into this world. My life was dedicated to science, and Dr. Lee had given me new purpose.

"He and I began meeting at his house several times a week. Mia was away finishing her degree, and Mrs. Lee mostly kept to herself. We would meet for hours in his basement lab, discussing ideas on how to literally solve the world's problems. That is where we designed our plan. It was outside the bounds of what Dr. Lee had proposed to the group. Originally, we were going to send a wake-up call to the world that would result in mass sickness. The H1N1 influenza as well as a number of other viruses were easily available and could have been dispersed in the same manner as our H3N7 virus. But Dr. Lee and I discussed it privately and we realized there would be only one chance to drastically change the course of humanity. The new plan had to result in death. Secretly, we and a few others began the long process of developing the H3N7 virus.

"Euthanasia has been used for centuries by man and nature to end a terminal illness or an incurable condition. From biblical, medieval, and modern times, both God and man have attempted to take on the challenge that we now undertake and both have failed. Floods, plagues, or mass executions never had any lasting corrective change. It is now our time to not just change man's destiny, but to control it.

"Before I go any further with our actual plan, Aubrey, we would like to hear your thoughts on what has thus far been presented," Mark said.

All eyes were on me.

My first reaction was to run like hell! I knew I wouldn't make it farther than the front door, so I smiled and gave a nod of acceptance. Life had given me my share of adversity. At times, I'd felt like my own fortress, protecting myself against invading aggressors. I'd managed to keep the gate barred up until that point and was not about to allow it to be opened then. I slowly made eye contact with each member of the group and finally settled my gaze on Mark.

"I wonder each day if things can get much worse, and by the end of the day, I'm assured they can," I said. "I have long given up on any promising direction for a positive global future. I fear I will never get a chance to experience life as it should be. I've long had a helpless feeling that mankind is destroying itself and that there is nothing I can do about it. As I witness man defile and contaminate the earth, it makes me feel ashamed to be part of the human species.

"Like you, I made a personal choice not to bring a child into this world. If you and this group have a plan to change this calamitous course, it would be my honor and duty to be part of it," I said, giving a good show of feeling passionate about the cause.

Mark was silent and expressionless, as was the rest of the group. No one made eye contact, and Mia was looking at the floor. This did not seem like a good sign. Maybe I'd gone a little too far, if that was even possible with a group of nuts like the ones in that room. Mark asked me if I would step out of the room and wait in the foyer. I nodded and exited the room. As I walked toward the entrance, I noticed the front door was blocked by two of the servant/guards. I sat in a chair by a statue of a Roman god and waited to learn my fate.

After about five minutes, which seemed more like an hour, Mark opened the door and asked me to return. I went back in and sat down in the chair I had previously occupied.

Mark began to speak. "Aubrey, I felt fate brought us together the day I first saw you at the antique market. I realized it when I walked in the door, and it was later confirmed when I heard your conversation with the customer. As you can imagine, recruiting you did not go over well. Bringing someone in at the eleventh hour, I admit, did not seem like a great idea. We certainly did not need any additional assistance to complete our mission, and it's always risky to expose our plan to anyone outside the core group, but I felt you were meant to be part of us.

"Dr. Lee sends his regrets that he has been unable to meet you, but he has full faith in my judgment and wanted me to welcome you to our cause. You are not the first to be brought in from outside our ranks. As you will soon find out, our networks extend across many organizations.

"We take no chances when it comes to recruitment. Everyone in this room has extensive knowledge about you and your background. We know that in high school you ran the 440 as a freshman and upset the favored senior in the state championship. We know your course curriculum when you attended Georgia College and State University and the names of all your friends and classmates. We know your religious and political beliefs as well as your habits and hobbies. We could probably tell you things about your life you have long forgotten. With us having studied that information, I convinced the group to allow me to present our mission to you and hear your thoughts. As you have probably deduced, you would not be back before us if we had not decided you were worthy of our cause. You may be joining us at the pinnacle of our plan, but nonetheless, you will play an important part." Mark sat down and waited for my response. It appeared that I had passed the first test, but I knew it all could fall apart and kept my reply short.

"*Thank you* is too mundane a reply for what you're allowing me to be a part of. At this point, I don't know exactly what your plans are, but I know drastic situations call for drastic measures. Consider me at your service," I said.

Mark and the others picked up glasses of champagne for a toast. I had not noticed that a flute was already sitting in front of me. These people seemed to have every detail analyzed and figured out. At least they thought they did.

The air in the room no longer seemed tense or anxious. We all talked like old friends. In my mind, I could picture myself walking up on the stage, in front of thousands, accepting my Oscar for Best Performance. Maybe I really did have a knack for theatrics. How ironic that I had been chosen for a part in a movie by people who had no intentions for me to ever act, and I might have just put on the best performance of my life.

"Aubrey, I'm having Walter bring you a dirty martini with pepper vodka and olives stuffed with blue cheese. I know it's your favorite drink, and you may need it as you hear our plan unfold. Let me warn you that you will be shocked, and we fully expect you to be. Believe us when we say we wish there were another way. There is no other way. Keep that in mind as I present it," Mark said.

I sat there calm and relaxed as Walter brought my drink. Thank God for the Xanax I'd found floating around at the bottom of my purse. It had been given to me by a friend after a few days filled with the kind of stress that a bottle of wine could not cure. Thankfully, I never got around to taking it then. But I'd swallowed it while wait-ing in the foyer and, within a few minutes, could feel the warming, calming effect as Mark continued.

"In less than thirty days, our biologically designed microorgan-ism will end the lives of about thirty million people," he said. "That is about ten percent of the US population. About thirty days later, it will take an additional ten million and have the entire world in chaos. The multitude of deaths that are a direct result of our actions will then have an ancillary effect that will greatly contribute to that number of lives lost. Global markets will shudder, and economic and political instability will reign. When we are ready, we will shut off the plague just as swiftly as it began and inform the leaders of the world that the population of the planet is in our hands.

"This is the basis of our plan; any questions or comments so far?" Mark asked with a cautionary tone.

Again, all eyes were on me and ready to gauge my reaction. I guessed this was phase two of my acceptance process. I knew that if I blinked, I would never leave the house alive. Earlier, I might have given the performance of my life; now I was to perform *for* my life.

"I'm not sure what reaction you're expecting, but if it's shock, you're not going to get it," I told the group. "As I said before, I've long lost any hope that mankind would survive its current direction. You made your point very clearly that man's intellectual corruptive nature could dramatically change the course of evolution, and I agree it needs to be corrected. But I've been let down before by big people selling big dreams. You've made a bold statement about changing the course of evolution. I've only heard the part about death and destruction, and you're not the first group to explore this concept. Before I get my hopes up, I would like to hear the rest of the plan," I said as I casually sipped my dirty martini.

I'm not sure Mark was prepared to divulge details of the plan, but after my commentary, he seemed to be put on the spot. I have no doubt he fully expected me to join the group, but I'm not so sure he expected me to be so audacious. He had no idea that the Xanax chased with champagne along with the martini had fueled me with uncharacteristic courage. I continued to stare at him, anticipating his response. He did a quick glance around the room, appearing to be unsure of his next move. Then he cleared his throat, punctuating his uneasiness. I half expected him to call for another summit and ask me to leave the room. After a few short seconds, he regained his composure and began to speak.

"My objective this evening was to introduce our group and our mission and provide you with the opportunity to join us. I'm relieved to avoid the unpleasantness of your possible refusal and can well see that you are committed to our cause. I see no reason not to expedite things and reveal the specific and technical particulars of our plan," Mark said.

I did not feel the need to speak, so I gave a slight nod and settled back in my seat. I was mentally preparing for what I was sure would be the most bizarre and insane ideas I would ever hear.

"H3N7 is the particular virus that will change the course of evolution and realign us in the proper direction," Mark began. "Its scientific relevance is as remarkable as the discovery of the human genome. We are the world's first scientists to develop and control the molecular dynamics of a virus. It is the common hemagglutinin and neuraminidase surface antigen. What we have done is mutate the virus and redesign its molecular structure. We increased the thickness of the viral envelope, making it impregnable to any chemical purification process. Its temperature tolerance is well outside any purification through heating or cooling. Under initial inspection, it will resemble the influenza virus and will be overlooked and disassociated with the cause of the mass death and destruction. Of course, with closer inspection it will reveal the biologically engineered virion, but at that point, it will be too late.

"What I have described up to now is manipulating a common virus into a super virus. I will next discuss the beauty and complexity of how we will introduce our creation. Do you have any questions at this point?" Mark asked.

I could not come close to imagining what would come next. It appeared that Mark and his group of megalomaniacs had created a Frankenstein virus, and I braced myself to hear the unfolding details. "No, I don't," I replied.

As Mark began to speak, his presence took on a strange transformation. I was staring into the face of evil. I was afraid that my pharmaceutical and cocktail courage was wearing off, and I could feel the anxiety beginning to take over.

"We stripped the virus of its own molecular genetic code and then took the H1N1 shell and designed a genetically altered virus," he said. "I would compare it to the process of surrogate parenting. We actually developed the H3N7 virus right here in Atlanta. One of our founding members is a top scientist with the Disease Control Center. Over the years, we recruited several biochemists from the DCC, allowing us full use of the most advanced laboratory in the world. I'm sure the irony has not escaped you—the greatest mass death since the Black Plague will have been financed by the taxes of the very people it will destroy. We think of this as evolutionary poetic justice," Mark stated with an arrogant smirk.

"It would take hours and three blackboards to explain the spectacular chemical equation. As much as I would love to roll up my sleeves and feel and smell the chalk in my hand, I will give you only the theoretical overview. Well, I say theoretical, but it is well beyond that. We did exhaustive animal testing, and though it may have been an ethical violation, we thoroughly tested the H3N7 virus on human subjects as well. There are a number of death row inmates that never made it to the chemical injection they were expecting. Our networks extend to the prison system, and what could be a better place to test H3N7? It is a controlled environment, and we get to administer a little of our own kind of justice. Ten subjects ingested the virus with water, and all ten exhibited or developed exactly the same symptoms. They all perished at precisely the same interval after ingestion and of the exact same complications. It was a magical experience to see it work perfectly to the minute most detail."

As I heard Mark's words, I could not believe this was actually happening. It seemed like we were at one of those Agatha Christie murder-mystery places where people act out roles and try to find out who the murderer is—which was not hard to figure out at this particular performance. Outwardly, I was nodding in agreement, and inwardly, I was screaming, *How in the hell did I get involved in this?* I realized at that moment I might in some way have the fate of the entire world in my hands. Me, Aubrey Reese from Jewell, Georgia! I build and refinish furniture, for God's sake. I don't poison millions of people.

I looked around the room to see the blank looks from the other members. I guessed if you'd been involved in that mess for most of your life, the speech was just one of many "Let's destroy the world" lectures you'd heard. I noticed Mia had been staring at me for quite some time. Was she seeing through my veiled façade? I could only wonder if the night and nightmare would ever end. I continued to concentrate on Mark's words and nodded my head in agreement, hoping that I passed for a fellow deranged zealot. Maybe they would give me a laminated membership card when the night was complete.

"H3N7 is the first virus to contain a chemically integrated schema," Mark continued. "It's basically programmed to follow a specific path and have a termination point. It's designed to terminate after nine days. We also added a redundant feature if for some reason the virus does not terminate after the initial infection period. As I stated before, H3N7 is impregnable to almost any cellular attack. We designed it to be vulnerable to only one, the acid located in the stomach.

"When H3N7 enters the stomach, it is activated by hydrochloric acid and the enzyme pepsin. It then travels to the small intestine where it mimics an amino acid and is transferred into the blood stream. It then goes through a translocation to its final destination, the brain.

"Once in the brain, it attacks the thalamus, located in the cerebral cortex. Over a period of twenty-four hours, the thalamus, which controls motor and sensory functions, is severely debilitated. On the second day, the affected person will enter a comatose state from which he will never recover. He will not perish for another seven days. This was designed to overwhelm the hospitals and health care systems. After the nine-day ordeal and ultimate death, H3N7 will terminate. If for some reason it were not to terminate, which I assure you it will, it could not survive without the live protein only found in a living thalamus. It would basically starve to death. This is how we control the virus," Mark said in a smug and arrogant tone.

He walked over toward the bar. Everyone seemed to be half asleep. He grabbed a bottle of water and took a long swig. He was enjoying the attention, although I was the only one who seemed to be watching. Mia was texting or doing something on her phone. How in the hell could this information become old hat? I could have heard it a thousand times and still have been traumatized. Mark screwed the cap back on the bottle and continued.

"Now, I will explain the method of delivery. On the same day and at the same precise time, sixteen ounces of the virus will be flushed into the water systems of seven major cities. The particular cities were chosen for their unique water purification and time-sensitive redistribution models. The billions of virions will disperse through the water systems and within days will end up in the municipal temporary holding ponds. The water will be treated in a series of vats. The purification process will strip and filter the water of all contaminates down to .5 microns. Viruses are measured in nanometers and are hundreds of times smaller than the .5 microns. They are usually killed by chemicals and the chlorination process—but of course, our virus will sustain and not be affected. After chlorination, sample tests will be taken, and the clean water will be approved again for human consumption.

"After the swirl of the vortex carries the fate of the world down the drain, the world will be changed forever. We will then take control.

"Our first order of business will be to inform and explain what has happened and that we are essentially holding the world hostage. With the ensuing chaos, the world leaders will have no choice but to submit to our demands. They will be desperate to comply. We will warn them that if we encounter any resistance, it will happen again—and on a much larger scale.

"Aubrey, the people you have met here tonight only scratch the surface of the reaches of our organization. We realized years ago that our gifts are in science and that we would need to recruit a matrix of political and economic leaders to help us take control of the world's affairs. Granted, most have only limited knowledge of the complexity of our plan, but they are totally committed to the outcome. After the collapse, it will all come together.

"Gone will be the greed to fill our pockets with gold while we destroy the earth's natural resources. No more plants and factories spewing toxins and pollutants, killing everything on land and in the oceans. We will control the population of the world and educate the masses to change their way of thinking. It may take thousands of years, but we will not fail in our conquest to save this planet! If there is a god, he will be very pleased with our efforts." Mark spoke with fervor as he shook his hands toward the ceiling.

I froze. Everyone had recovered from their slumber and was keenly watching Mark as he preached to the room. Mia put her phone away and was watching me, ready to gauge any visible reaction. I did not have one. I was so shocked at what I was hearing I could not move. To borrow an old country expression, these people were crazier than a shit-house rat! I had read and heard about psychopaths before, but I had never been around any, and especially not a room full of them.

How could they believe this stuff? How could they have not been caught? And Mia! How could she function like a normal person and be working for the fucking FBI?

Maybe there was no virus and everything was a figment of their imaginations. Maybe they ate mushrooms every few months and acted out this mad-scientist, take-over-the-world shit. Whatever the case, I had to appear to drink the Kool-Aid if I wanted to get out of there alive.

Mark wiped the sweat off his forehead, took a deep breath, and continued.

"The seven cities and the seven people to deliver the H3N7 have been chosen. They are the seven people in this room."

I only counted six people and wondered who the seventh "chosen one" could be. I then noticed Walter the bartender in the corner of the room. Hell, why not? He could have a PhD in astrophysics for all I knew. Mark continued with his madness and laid out the rest of the plan.

"The cities to be cleansed first are the locations of our current movie production sites. They are Los Angeles, San Francisco, New York, Portland, Des Moines, Atlanta, and Dallas. As previously arranged, I will take Los Angeles, and Thomas will deliver San Francisco. Jason has Dallas, and Francis, Portland. Walter goes to Des Moines, and Mia will take New York, which leaves Atlanta for Aubrey," Mark instructed.

Well, looking on the bright side, I did not have to travel far to kill my millions of people. I could not help but find some sort of gallows humor in something that seemed so far-fetched and unreal. My mind was incapable of accepting what it heard. I was confident that in the next few hours I would have a panic attack and a nervous breakdown, but at the moment, I could only see Mark's plan as the subject of a Vince Flynn novel.

—

The evening was growing long, and I was dreading what would happen after Mark's speech. He continued. "Our method of delivery is simple and foolproof. Seven vans marked with studio logos will depart the estate, headed for their respective sites. The West Coast vans will leave three days early and travel across the country. In each of the seven vans will be one of us and a company driver. The vans will be loaded with video and technical equipment. Our H3N7 will be among the cargo items. The method for disguising the virus is quite ingenious. I must give credit to Mia for coming up with the idea," Mark said.

I looked over at Mia, and she gave a slight nod and a smile to the group. She seemed quite proud of her idea. I was still waiting for her to pull the coup de grâce and rat me out, but so far she had remained silent.

"For each city, we've filled two eight-ounce glass-cleaner bottles with the liquid emulsifier containing the virus. We then added isopropanol alcohol, ammonia, and a blue dye. If used, the solution would actually clean glass. To prevent accidental use, the nozzles will be secured in the off position. The two bottles for each city will be enclosed in a lens-cleaning kit with other supplies. In three days, the first vans will leave for their destinations. Ten days from now will be another day that some will say will live in infamy. History will eventually prove this wrong and declare it a day of celebration of the new direction of evolutionary man.

"My friends, that day will be March thirty first, Easter Sunday. None of us are religious in a traditional way, but we certainly know God never intended man to be on this course of greed and corruption. I believe we are disciples of God, and he has ordained us to carry out this mission," Mark said emphatically.

As he spoke, I saw for the first time in my life something I've always heard about but never experienced. Behind Mark was a wall painted eggshell white. Emitting from the crown of Mark's head was an almost black halo that seemed to go at least a foot up the wall. It was an evil aura and very frightening, and it appeared that no one else could see it. When he brought up the part about the idea having been ordained by God, it flashed like a black bolt of lightning. He was correct about the plan having being ordained; it just hadn't been ordained by God.

Every minute brought a new twist and element of surprise. I was deeply concerned. If I did manage to get out of that house alive, what action could I possibly take to prevent the madness? Who would believe me, and what proof did I have?

Yes, officer, I attended a cocktail and dinner party at one of the most prestigious addresses in Atlanta, and they were telling me how they plan to destroy mankind by killing millions of people and then taking over the world. There is an FBI agent and a top scientist from the Centers for Disease Control involved in the plan.

They would promptly throw me in the nuthouse, and I would not blame them. As I contemplated this, I noticed Mark look at his watch, and I guessed he was about to wrap things up.

"I want you all to go home and get your affairs in order," he said. "Our mission will take seven days, and then we will locate back in Atlanta for an indefinite time. We will set up our command post here at the estate. As you all know, we have two floors underground with a complete laboratory. After H3N7 is dispensed into the water systems, everyone is to immediately return to the estate. We will monitor the progress of the virus from our media center. We have all discussed the action plan for our families and will coordinate the plan upon our return. At the proper time, we will inform the world what has taken place and outline the future. Our leaders will take their places, and our recovery will begin.

"Unless necessary, I will not be in contact with anyone from this point until we meet back here in three days at 1700 hours. At that point, we will leave for our individual cities. Rest well over the next few days; it will be the last rest you will get for a very long time."

I was standing there not sure what to do. Was I simply to walk out of there, get into my car, and head back to Porterdale? There is nothing in the world I would have welcomed more than to see those damn cats and that piece-of-shit RV. But that was not to be. Mark and Mia were walking my way.

"Aubrey, I'm going to be occupied here at the estate and won't be able to guide you through your training. Mia has volunteered to take my place and will give you further instructions and assist you in your responsibilities. If either of you needs me, I prefer you come to the estate. I'm going to limit my cell phone use and will be hard to reach," Mark said.

"Don't worry about us," Mia said. "We'll map out the Atlanta implementation sites and make a few dry runs. In the next day or so, I will show her the bottom floors of the estate and her quarters on the second floor," Mia said with confidence.

Mark said goodbye and walked over to a few of the other guests, or maybe I should say *cult members*. Mia motioned for us to walk outside and leave the gathering. We walked down the drive and sat in a small garden area located just off the driveway. It had a wonderful four-tiered water fountain with a statue of some goddess at the top. The sound of the water would have been soothing in almost any other situation.

"We have a lot to accomplish over the next couple of days. Are you sure you are committed and ready to assume your responsibilities?" Mia asked. I was sure this was a rhetorical question. She, of course, knew there was only one answer I could give.

"I'm ready and have no concerns in carrying out my part of the plan," I replied.

Mia sat silently and cast her eyes toward the lights of the fountain. After a few moments, she faced me with a stern expression and said, "You're lying." She stood up and walked a few steps toward me. As she reached into her purse and removed a small, dark object, she said, "You may think you put on a good show in there, but you failed miserably."

At that point, I expected the worst.

I could feel the heat flash from my head through my body and cover me like a smothering blanket. The impact to my chest took my breath away. Sheer fear and panic had taken over. I knew my life and future were held by the person sitting in front of me. Her stare was unwavering and seemed to last a lifetime. There were no words for me to say, even if I'd been capable of speaking them. We heard voices coming from the front entry of the house, and the sound broke Mia's stare. She glanced over that way and then back at me. I wanted to look over my shoulder at what I assumed were the guards coming to get me, but I was unable to make the effort.

"What you failed to realize is that the chair you were sitting in was wired with a heart and heat monitoring system. It was interfaced with a software program that is the most sophisticated lie detection program available. Again, I don't have to tell you that you failed it miserably," Mia said as she turned off the power to her cell phone. "Never can be too sure about these things," she said as she returned the phone to her purse.

I knew I was not out of the woods, but at least I could draw a breath. The thought had never crossed my mind that they would have a damn lie detector. Although it really would not have mattered; the outcome would have been the same. I suddenly realized that Mark was unaware of my lies. I wondered what Mia's angle was.

"Fortunately for you, I had control of the computer and administered the test," she said. "I also reported the findings when you were out of the room. I had previously prepared a passing report and presented it to the group. Had I given the actual results, you would have never returned to that room, and—well, you know the rest," she said with a slightly smug tone.

I did not know whether to hug her or slap the shit out of her. I decided slapping her was probably not a good idea. I still did not know what to say, and she sensed it.

"I think it's time I do some explaining," she said as she returned to her seat on the bench. "Needless to say, I'm terribly sorry you've been exposed to all this. As you are now aware, I did not have a choice. Mark was smitten with you from the first time he saw you at the antique market. We desperately tried to talk him out of involving you, but he would not listen.

"As you witnessed tonight, he believes he has been ordained by some higher power and that nothing can stop him. As this thing gets closer to becoming reality, his arrogance, aligned with his emotional instability, has caused him to become very reckless. He seemed to have lost his senses even further when it came to you. There was so much contention within the group that at one point I thought the plan would be put on hold, but unfortunately, no one had to courage to confront Mark. The last thing I needed was a civilian getting in my way. I had my hands full and did not need another distraction. But as things have unfolded, you have actually been a godsend. Not just for the FBI, but maybe for me personally," Mia said with relief in her voice.

I finally regained my composure and began to ask a few questions. "I'm really confused. You grew up around all this delusional, dysfunctional craziness, and both your parents were devoted to the cause. Your whole childhood, education, career path, and life have been structured by the ideals of this group. From what I heard tonight, the implementation of the plan that will kill millions of people is right around the corner. At what point did you decide it was not such a good idea?" I asked with a little attitude.

"True, I did grow up with the ideals and philosophies of everyone in the room tonight. I was homeschooled and spent most of my time around the group and the Georgia Tech campus. I did not have other kids to play with and became an adult at an early age. I knew no ideology other than my parents' beliefs. My peers were my pseudo aunts and uncles, and they had the same screwed-up ideas as my parents. At the time, I did not realize the rest of society did not think the same way. I remained reclusive throughout college, studied constantly, and had perfect grades. When at school, I was always in contact with and cared for by my parents or someone in the group. I was shy and did very little socializing. I know it sounds like I was being indoctrinated into the Hitler Youth, but it was not like that. Everyone in the group had their lives and careers, and the discussions at the meetings were more academic and theoretical. There was no master plan to end civilization—at least not back then.

"Things started to change ten years ago when my mother died. We were not very close, but toward the end, she began to open up to me and express her concerns. She did not like the current direction of the group. She told me that Mark and my father were beginning to take things to a new level. As I later found out, my dad came up with the idea of the virus, and Mark was immediately all in. I'm not sure what caused my father to go off the deep end. Maybe he was always a psycho, and I just never realized it.

"Together, they fueled the fire of the group's already wild ideas and convinced them to adopt the plan. Had they not needed the resources of the group, they would have probably proceeded on their own. The two of them were inseparable, and Mark was the son my father never had. Because of our culture, he expected me to be subservient and never saw me as an individual. I think the only reason I was allowed to be part of the family was to satisfy my mother's maternal ambitions." Mia looked at the ground, and I could see the rejection by her father had left its mark. It saddened me to think of the coldness with which people sometimes treated others with little or no concern about the impacts of their actions.

We continued to sit in the little garden, and I was a bit concerned that we were staying too long and having our discussion too close to the house. The guests had left, and I assumed Mark had retired for the evening or was in the lab with his beloved virus. I expressed this concern to Mia, and she let out a little laugh.

"I actually have a room here, and when I used to stay overnight, I would spend most of the evenings here in this garden. I've rarely been back since beginning the investigation. I can only take so many chances. As for the surveillance system, I designed it, and there is no audio or video equipment nearby, so we are safe to stay and talk as long as we want. Are you in a hurry to get back to the RV?" she asked with a teasing smile.

"Is that where I'm going?" I asked.

"I'm not sure yet. I haven't thought that far ahead."

We left the fountain area, walked further into the garden, and stopped near a small pond, where Mia continued with her explanation.

Chapter Twelve

Mia

It wasn't an easy story to tell. It was personal—and painful.

Even my mother never knew the things I was telling Aubrey, and for that, at least, I was grateful. Before her death, she did become aware of the new direction things were heading in, but thankfully she never knew about the virus or the ultimate plan for the massive sweep of deaths. It would have given me much pain to think that she went to her grave carrying that burden. Things had changed around our house, and my dad had basically shut her out of his life. I would come home on holidays to find him locked up in his basement lab and my mom withdrawn and seemingly depressed. It was only a few months later that she became sick. She was diagnosed with a rare form of leukemia and, despite all the treatments, died within a year. I will always believe that the worry contributed to her illness. I wish I'd spent more time with her.

As I poured my feelings out to Aubrey, I began to cry and after a few moments collected myself.

Shortly after my mother's death, I finished my degree at the University of Virginia and was recruited by the FBI. My father was very pleased and encouraged me to take the job. After Mom's death, he began taking more of an interest in my life, and I was delighted to have his attention. Mark and I became closer as well. It was comforting to have the support of my family, especially with my mother gone. I accepted the job with the bureau and spent the first year mostly training and getting used to the protocols of law enforcement. I was assigned to a position in the Atlanta office and started my new life. When not at work, I mostly kept to myself.

After the first year or so, Mark and I began spending more time together, and he slowly started bringing me into the group. I would attend a meeting every few months. I had known most of the group since early childhood, and it was always good to see them and catch up.

Everything remained fairly normal until late 2010. I began to notice a sense of urgency developing with Mark and my dad. The meetings became more frequent, and the dialogue and mood began to change. One evening in late December, Mark and my father asked me to stick around after the meeting. I remember the uneasy feeling I got in my stomach wondering what was about to take place. I knew it was not going to be good.

They gathered with me in the foyer, and we all walked into Mark's large private study. The walls were lined with exotic animals that had been killed somewhere near the far reaches of the earth. I knew that Mark had not hunted them, and I always wondered who had been responsible for the senseless deaths of such beautiful animals. It was a powerful distraction, and I was thinking that was probably the point. Mark always wanted to control the moment.

"'Mia, we brought you in tonight because we need your help.' My father addressed me as I was sitting in a chair studying the head of a giraffe. "Things are starting to happen that you need to be aware of. The law enforcement community, namely your employer, is starting to take an increased interest in groups like ours. You are aware of this, aren't you?' he asked.

The answer was that I was indeed aware; I'd been assigned to work in counter terrorism.

"Yes, I am," I told him, "but as far as I know, this group, which doesn't even have a name, is not on any list."

"'If we are not, that's great, but I would expect that to change real soon. When it does, we need you to deflect as much attention from us as you can. Can you do that for us?" My father had walked over and sat down in a chair next to mine and put his arm around me. "We really need you to step up and become an integral part of the group. We need you to help us with the bureau as well as assisting us in finishing the last phase of our plan. What do you say, my little girl? Will you help us?" he asked, as if I were ten years old and he needed me to clean the dishes and then clean my room.

Of course I said yes. What other answer was there than yes? I still did not know exactly what was going on and could somewhat honestly play that card for a while. But I knew deep in my soul that I was about to find out information that would blow that claim to innocence out of the water.

Mark walked over from the bar with three drinks in hand. They were all some type of brown liquor that seemed to be mixed with an effervescent. He handed one to each of us and sat down. He looked at my father and asked, "Do you want to explain it or shall I?"

My father had a tired, overworked expression and said in a quiet voice, "I think you should."

Over the next hour, Mark explained to me much of the plan. I stayed calm and went with what they were saying but was freaking out inside. I could not imagine that the people I had known all my life were capable of mass homicide and destruction. It all seemed like a cruel fantasy world with no connection to reality. But it was real. I had no idea they had created—or were even capable of creating—the virus they described. I must have really had my head under a rock not to have seen this coming. How in the world could I return to work knowing what I now knew? Well, that was exactly what Mark and my dad expected me to do. They expressed how proud they were of me and how I would be a hero to the world when one day the story was told—and that would be soon!

I was tired and shocked and just wanted to go to bed. Mark insisted I stay in my room at the estate and said that we would discuss things further in the morning. He said things would look a lot better then. I guess even a psychopath can be an optimist.

I drug myself upstairs and passed out in bed. Luckily, I was off the next day, or I would have had to call in sick. I was in no shape to face the bureau then, if I ever would be.

—

Aubrey and I walked back from the small pond to the benches by the fountain. I could tell her mind was blown, but there was more to tell. We both sat down and were silent for several minutes as I twisted a rope bracelet on my wrist.

Finally, I began again.

I explained that only a few months after Mark filled me in on what was going on, our little group did indeed become of interest to the FBI. It appeared that Mark had attempted to obtain some information over the internet that had placed him on the radar of

Homeland Security and the FBI. If invasion of privacy ever had its merits, it definitely did in this case. It was a search involving the details of the municipal water systems in multiple states. He was looking for water systems that moved purified water directly back to the public instead of being stored in tanks for indefinite periods. The seven cities he mentioned were not chosen at random. They were all using a new innovative "green" technology that takes wastewater and converts it directly into tap water. Most of the country was experiencing drought conditions at the time, and this process conserves water and energy by not having to treat the water multiple times or store it. It's a very efficient system, but by speeding up and localizing the process, it also makes a convenient target for terrorists. That's why the FBI and Homeland Security were monitoring internet searches on the topic.

I immediately went into a panic when our boss informed us that we were to initiate an investigation. I think I turned pale and nearly passed out when she assigned it to me, although it was not a high-priority assignment, more of a fact-finding mission. We had things like this pop up on our radar every day that never panned out to be anything.

The first thing I did after that meeting was to call Mark. Of course, he had me come over that evening to discuss the situation. He explained that things were not that dire and that he had assumed the group would eventually fall under the suspicion of the FBI. He felt that it was an act of fate that I was in control of the investigation.

On the way home, I decided that Mark might be right and that fate had indeed played an important role in how things were falling into place. It was almost like my whole life had prepared me for this event. I made the decision that I would not deny fate and would play my part in the production—only it would not be the part Mark and my father had planned for me.

—

I felt strong, like I could do it, I told Aubrey. Because something had happened to me not long before that had made me a different person.

I glanced over at her. At last, I could tell her something good, about an unexpected gift that had come into my life in the midst of all the chaos. A sense of peace began to chip away at the hard knot in my chest.

"Aubrey, my life changed a few months before the meeting with Mark and my dad," I said. "Something happened that was totally foreign to me and like nothing I had ever experienced. It was the signal that clearly showed me that this world was a beautiful and wonderful place, a sign that things were not meant to be controlled or guided in a particular direction, that there was a balance in life and everything was happening as it should."

Aubrey watched me closely. "What was the change?" she asked.

I suddenly felt shy. "I fell in love," I told her. It changed everything. I began to see things through a much different view. I had hope for the future and realized that most people in this world share a common compassion and love for one another. Love is not an order of evolution—it's a gift from God, and what a precious gift. I wake up every day thankful for finally finding it."

She asked the question that I knew that she would: "Who is this love?"

I was feeling sheepish and yet full of warmth, almost forgetting for a moment we were a hundred yards from a virus intended to kill half the world.

"Agent John Holmes," I told her.

"I guess I should've known from the way that you look at him," she said, then paused. "Does he know about your involvement and history with the group?"

That's when the peace and warmth turned into coldness. Because the answer was he didn't.

CHAPTER THIRTEEN

Aubrey

I could already see the writing on the wall. Not only was Mia expecting me to assist her in foiling the plan, but she also wanted me to help her explain everything to John. I'm certainly not well versed in relationship advice, but it looked like I didn't have a choice. I had to really think things through and hopefully guide her with the correct advice. If things didn't go well with John, it would not end with her simply going home with a quart of ice cream and crying herself to sleep; it could trigger world destruction. With all of her educational degrees, it was obvious that she had very little knowledge about affairs of the heart.

"Aubrey, will you please help me figure out how to tell John?" she asked with tears in her eyes. I moved next to her and gave her a reassuring hug. "Of course I will," I said. "There's always a true test when it comes to love, and this will be one hell of a test. I'm sure he will listen and understand the pressure you've been under, especially if we hold a gun on him and handcuff him to a chair," I added with a laugh.

Mia smiled and nodded while wiping her tears. As daunting a task as we faced in saving the world from the horrible ills of Mark and his group, all Mia was thinking about right then was making things right with John. Love is powerful, and who knows? Maybe it does conquer all.

In the darkness, we slipped back though the garden sitting area and found our cars. I followed Mia up the driveway and gave the gatehouse attendant a small wave as we passed. He smiled and waved back. I wondered if he knew what was taking place just a few hundred feet away.

Mia insisted that I stay with her, and I did not argue. I was too exhausted to drive back to Porterdale and deal with the cats and the stink in the RV. As I followed Mia back to her Buckhead condo, I could not help but think of the conversation that lay ahead with John. My thoughts drifted to possible scenarios, and I had to slam on my brakes to avoid hitting a car that had gotten between me and Mia.

I turned on the radio in an attempt to ease my mind and relax. Prince was singing "1999," a song that was a little too prophetic and that put my focus right back on our doomsday situation. It had been a long, stressful day and I would be glad to see it come to a close. Mia, just ahead of me, was turning into her condo parking lot. Finally, we'd arrived, and I could see a large glass of red wine in my near future.

We pulled side by side into a pair of parking places, and Mia quickly jumped out of her car. As I was getting out of my Jeep, she approached me with a troubled expression on her face.

"That's John's car," she said, pointing toward a black Suburban a few spaces away. "I didn't tell him where I would be tonight, and he's called several times. He left a couple of messages asking where I was and saying we needed to talk. He was supposed to be out with a few friends, and we hadn't planned on seeing each other until tomorrow. Oh, Aubrey, I think he knows something's wrong!" she exclaimed.

Well, it was about time he figured out something was wrong, I thought. His last name seemed to be the only similarity he had to the famous English detective. I knew Mia had not been very forthcoming with John about her past, but I was wondering how he had yet to make the connection with Mark. But love is both trusting and blind. It leads us to believe the best about people, and sometimes we choose not to see what is right in front of us.

"Mia, I don't think we're prepared to tell John about your past. We only have one chance, and we need to discuss how to present it. Maybe we should run down to Fado's bar and drink this thing out," I said anxiously.

The suggestion had barely left my mouth when she jumped into my car, ready to go. Within six minutes, we were at the Irish pub.

"A bottle of Chateauneuf du Pape and two large Bordeaux glasses," Mia told the server. We both were silent and stared around the room as we waited on the wine. The server arrived and began to do the usual song and dance with the cork and tasting. Before he got started, we both nodded our approval and in unison said, "Pour."

With a full glass of wine, I offered up a toast. "Here's to the two men in our life. From one, we want approval, and from the other, we want removal," I said, laughing a little as we clinked our glasses. "Okay, time to hear about you and John. Take it from the beginning."

Mia took a deep breath and began.

"John and I were recruited into the same training class in 2003. There had been a flurry of terrorism around the world, and it had just been two years since nine-eleven. Every recruit wanted to be placed into a counter-terrorism unit. I was one of the top recruits and, after completing our training, pretty much had my choice of assignments. Atlanta seemed to be everyone's choice, and there was only one position open. Only one obstacle stood in my way, the physical fitness standards. I would have ended up in some basement cubicle staring at a computer if I hadn't greatly improved my field fitness abilities. That's how John came into my life. He was top in the class when it came to the PT standards, but with a college degree in exercise science, he didn't have the mindset of a counter-terrorism agent. He was afraid he wouldn't pass the exams to qualify for the unit. We made a deal and became close friends. He would teach me how to get over those damn ten-foot walls and crawl under eight-inch barbed wire, and I would tutor him for the CT placement exams."

"And it looks like your plan worked," I said.

She smiled. "Six months later, we were both successful in passing all our exams and were both placed into counter-terrorism units. I chose Atlanta to be closer to my family, and he was assigned to Washington, DC. We had very little contact until he was transferred to Atlanta in 2009. He joined our unit, and I was very happy to be reunited with him. Then something happened that changed everything."

"What happened?" I eagerly asked.

"In June of that year, our unit was alerted that a large supply of fertilizer had been stolen from a distributor in Davisboro, Georgia. Davisboro is a small town about two hours southeast of Atlanta. Reginald Dent, the owner of the company, reported the theft of over fifteen thousand pounds of nitrogen fertilizer. That is the same type of fertilizer that was used in the bombing of the federal building in Oklahoma City. The theft had occurred the previous night, and we knew the only way to transport that much fertilizer was by tractor and trailer. We set up a surveillance of everything within three hundred miles from the Davisboro location. That was the maximum distance the truck could have traveled in that time frame. We had a hunch they would be headed toward Atlanta and alerted all law enforcement along the I-20 corridor.

"The hunch paid off when the rig was spotted at a small truck stop near the town of Crawfordville, about an hour east of Atlanta. As soon as we were notified, our unit was dispatched, and we were on our way to intercept the truck and hopefully the crew. John and I were the first to arrive and were received by two Taliaferro County deputy sheriffs. We remained at a safe distance from the truck as we sized up the situation and waited on the rest of our unit. The truck was parked on the side of the lot near a patch of trees. There were no other vehicles near the truck, and it appeared it had been abandoned. It was the type of truck that didn't have a sleeping unit, and checking with binoculars, I thought the cab looked unoccupied."

I could tell that nothing good would be coming next. Mia paused to take a drink and briefly closed her eyes against the memory of that day.

"We decided to drive around the truck and take a closer look," she said. "John wanted to inspect the truck and trailer to see if the cargo was still there. I told him to wait. I reminded him we needed to follow protocol and not engage until the rest of our unit arrived. Things did not seem right, and I felt we were missing something. But John was impatient and told me he was just going to take a quick walk around the rig. Before I could officially tell him not to engage, he jumped out of the Suburban. He drew his Beretta .40 S&W handgun and approached the front of the truck. I noticed he was not wearing his Armorlite protection vest. He had gotten ahead of himself, and I stepped out of the SUV to warn him of his error and order him back into the vehicle.

I took a sip of wine and leaned forward eagerly.

"I had only taken a few steps," she continued, "when I realized I was squinting from the sun and had to shield my eyes. This was dangerous, and I was turning to retrieve my sunglasses when a shadow blocked out the sun. I did not have to think about it—I knew what it was. John realized it as well, but a second too late. The men had been lying flat on top and in the middle of the trailer. With the way the truck was angled in relation to the parking lot, it had been impossible to see them. They must have seen the deputy sheriff arrive and been unable to escape. One of the men had spotted John getting too close and sprung up from the top of the truck. He had a military-style automatic rifle aimed right at John. Unable to react, John waited on the hail of bullets."

"Oh, Mia," I said, unable to imagine the horror that she must have felt.

She picked up her glass, but simply stared at the liquid that swirled inside. It was as if she had forgotten the bar and the wine; her mind was far away at a dusty truck stop where bullets would be flying any moment. "As soon as I saw the shadow, I immediately pulled my Sig Sauer handgun and raised it toward the sky," she said. "You can tell the second that someone is about to pull the trigger of a gun. Their whole body slows down just a bit, and they become rigid for a millisecond. You can almost sense their brain sending the impulse to their finger. I was about a quarter of a second ahead of the guy. I fired my weapon and hit him square in the chest. As soon as he was hit, the impulse reached his finger and an involuntary round went just above John's head, burrowing into the pavement behind him. I put down the second guy as soon as he came into sight," Mia said as she swirled her glass of wine.

"So what happened was that I saved John's life that day. We formed a very close bond after that, which is not uncommon when one partner saves the other's life. We began to have lunch and spend more time together, and I could tell he wanted it to be more. I was a little tentative and cautious about seeing him—the stuff with Mark and the group was hanging over my head."

Then the smallest of smiles began to break up the darkness on her face. "He finally won me over with a dog," she explained. "I was absolutely helpless when he asked me to accompany him to the animal shelter to pick out a puppy. After hugging and squeezing half the dogs, we settled on a little black lab. He named him Sig, and from that point on, John, Sig, and I were inseparable. We spent most evenings together . . . and then it extended to overnights. I was a little worried that our relationship might be temporary, stemming from that emotional day at the truck stop, but after a few months, I knew our love was genuine."

We sat there in silence for a few minutes and finished our wine. I was thinking about the bizarre circumstances that had brought Mia and John together. I guess some people find love in the produce section, and some find it in the aftermath of a terrorist shootout. I had no doubt those two were in love, but love is always put to a test, and sometimes it fails. I finally stood up, took a deep breath, and pointed toward the door. It was time for the test.

—

We arrived back at the condo and, of course, John's vehicle was still there. As much as I wanted to fall into a deep slumber, it seemed I still had a few hours to go to fulfill the plans that destiny had set out for me that day. Mia's shoulders slumped, and I could see the resignation in her eyes. Neither of us wanted a confrontation with

John, but of course we had no choice. The time of reckoning was just a few minutes away, and my stomach was fluttering. I gave her a big hug and told her everything would be all right. Funny thing, but I really believed it. I had no doubt John would be overwhelmed—who wouldn't be?—but when your heart is true, and your intentions are pure, the power of love can scale almost any obstacle.

We walked up the steps to the door, and Mia inserted her key and unlocked it. Entering the room, the first thing we saw was John sitting on the couch. He did not make a move and watched us as we approached him. It was a tense and awkward moment. I didn't know whether to sit, stand, or what. Mia appeared to be unsure as well.

John broke the silence and suggested we both sit down.

As much as I hated small talk, I would have loved nothing more than to discuss the weather or the Braves' upcoming spring training.

It was not to be. John's next words were, "Mia, I need to know what's going on."

Mia glanced in my direction, hoping I would save her. I could not. It was time to explain everything to John. She dropped her head and began to cry. Her long black hair covered her face and hid the anguish she was feeling.

John sensed this and went to her side. He put his arms around her, pulling her close, and told her everything was going to be all right.

"No, it won't! You'll never be able to forgive me," Mia said through tearful sobs.

"Mia, there's nothing we can't face or work out together. You're the best thing that has ever happened to me, and I'll stand by you no matter what. Please tell me what's happened," John said with tears in his eyes.

Mia just collapsed in his arms and could not stop crying. I could feel the tears running down my face as well. I had decided to find the guest room and leave the daunting dilemma to the two of them, but before I could make my escape, John looked my way. "Aubrey, since Mia's too upset to talk, can you please tell me what's going on?" he softly asked.

I immediately thought, *Damn it, man!* This was not my story to tell. I was a late-in-the-game casualty and still looking for answers myself. It was the same old story—friend gets involved, friend gets thrown under the proverbial bus. But I knew there was no way I was going to get out of it, and I decided to jump right in. Hopefully, Mia would eventually regain her composure and take over.

"John, it's a bizarre, long, complicated story that's quite unbelievable, and I'm having a terrible time comprehending it myself. It would be much better if Mia could tell you." I made one last attempt to get her engaged.

John looked over at Mia, who was still crying, then back at me. "I have a strong suspicion it involves Mark McClure," he said.

"To the core," I answered.

Mia let out a loud wail at the mention of Mark's name and grabbed her stomach and disappeared into the bathroom.

At that point, I knew for sure I would be the one explaining things, but first, I had a few questions for John. I moved from my chair to the couch across from him, and for a few moments, we just stared at each other. It was obvious that I would have to start the conversation.

"You and Mia have been close for almost two years. Are you just now having suspicions about any history between Mia and Mark?" I incredulously asked.

John just sat there with a blank expression. I could not read him one way or the other.

"You must think I am a terrible FBI agent . . ."

"Well, the thought has certainly crossed my mind," I answered. John sat up straighter on the edge of the couch and took a second to collect his thoughts. "The truth is, I know more than you suspect. At least I think I do," he replied. "Early on, I could sense a small amount of stress when Mia had to report on the activities of Mark and his organization. No one else could see it, but she and I spent a lot of time together, and I was pretty good at reading her emotions. I didn't think much of it at first, but as the group became more active and our investigation increased, she became more anxious. About a month ago, I started to dig around. I figured Mia must have had some history from a case involving a member of the group. I could not find a connection in the FBI or any law enforcement files, so I did the next best thing and Googled them. It's amazing what you can find if you ask the right questions. I discovered that Mark and most of the group had attended Georgia Tech at the same time. I accessed the university's School of Biology's archives and searched McClure's name. I found a published piece he wrote right after receiving his doctorate. The co-author was Dr. Lee.

"Mia had told me her father was a retired professor from Georgia Tech, but with the different last name, and with Dr. Lee never being on our watch list, I was slow to put it together. I did a faculty search on Dr. Lee, and it led me to his biography. There on the page was an outdated photo of Dr. and Mrs. Lee and Mia. She was much younger, but her name was listed, and I could easily tell it was her. The article was a disturbing piece on the direction of evolution and what would happen if something didn't change. It did not go as far as to offer any suggestions, but it implied something drastic needed to happen. I'm not sure what's going on, but I suspect Mia's somehow involved. I've been waiting a week or so to confront her," John said with a sigh.

I stood corrected on my assessment of John's sleuthing. I was actually very impressed with his patience and how he had handled the situation. If he had brought this to the attention of anyone at the bureau, there was a good chance Mia would be sitting in jail and that Mark and his crowd would have gone underground. I was also relieved that John was at least partially aware of what was happening and we were not having to explain everything from scratch. I really needed Mia to come out of the bathroom and join the discussion, but before I could get up and try and coax her out, John hit me with a question.

"Where were you and Mia tonight? Mia hasn't updated me since our last meeting, and with you sitting here tonight, I feel like something important has happened."

I suspected that Mia was no longer sick, if she ever had been, and probably had her ear pressed to the door, hanging on our every word. I wanted to jerk her out of the bathroom and make her explain things to John, but it was apparent she was not going to be of any help. I took a long breath before going down what I feared might be the road of no return.

"You're going to have to promise that you will sit there and listen to everything I have to say," I told John. "As I said before, what's taking place is bizarre and unbelievable but—trust me—very real. I'm caught up in this mess way more than you can imagine, and Mia and I really need you right now."

"Aubrey, I'm expecting the worst, and I have already prepared myself. I know Mia's in trouble and is probably involved way over her head. I will do whatever it takes to help her. She saved my life, and it's my turn to save hers," John replied.

As the old expression goes, this was where the rubber met the road. I was not going to withhold the slightest detail. I fully expected Mia to pass out and hit the floor when I brought up the subject of H3N7.

It took me about an hour to explain Mia's involvement, from the time she was a mere child to her placement with the FBI. It took an additional hour to explain in the briefest of terms the dynamics and creation of the H3N7 virus and what the group had planned. I'm not sure what I expected John's reaction to be, but he just sat there, locked in a trance. He had just *thought* he was prepared for the worst.

I must admit I felt a sense of empowerment. Here I had one federal agent scared to come out of the bathroom and the other thrown into a state of shock by the news I'd just delivered. I was the only rational person in the condo, and it was time for me to take further control. I got up and marched over to the bathroom and yanked the door open. Damned if Mia was not laying there curled up in a ball. The time for sensitivity was over.

"Mia, get your ass up and come see about John. As I'm sure you've heard, he now knows the whole story. It's time to start acting like an FBI agent. I'm done. I'm going to go upstairs, take a hot bath, get into bed, and hopefully wake up tomorrow morning in Madison, realizing this was all a bad dream."

—

The next morning, I woke to the sound of voices, and to my dismay, they belonged to John and Mia—so much for all this being a horrible dream.

I pulled myself from the bed, took a quick glance in the mirror, and descended the stairs to the kitchen. John and Mia were sitting at the breakfast table talking. They stopped as I entered the room. Mia had dark circles under her eyes, and John looked exhausted. I assumed they had been up all night reconciling the recent events.

They were both drinking coffee, and upon seeing me, John slowly moved to the kitchen and returned with another cup. I pulled up a chair and sat down. They were both initially silent and stared into their coffee. I can only imagine what the night had been like for them, and I was sure they were worn out and tired of talking. But when John looked up, I could tell I was wrong. He appeared to be searching for the right words to continue the conversation.

Finally, he began. "Aubrey, Mia and I don't quite know what to say. Not only as agents but also as your friends, we cannot thank you enough for helping us. You bridged the gap that Mia and I would have found difficult, if not impossible, to get over on our own. You could have easily walked away from this debacle and never looked back. From talking to Mia, it's apparent that if things had not worked out last night, you would have never left that place alive. We can never thank you enough for your courage and your commitment."

Listening to John recount my most recent decisions was frightening. If I had taken the time to weigh the risks I had faced the night before, I'm not sure I would have had the courage to follow through. But I think there are times in our lives when we recognize that the greater good is larger than ourselves. What's ironic is that from an evolutionary perspective, it was counterintuitive for me to voluntarily walk into the face of danger. It was purely my spiritual nature guiding my altruistic behavior.

I could feel the heavy emotion in the room and was ready to change the mood and get everyone focused on our task. "So where do we go from here?" I asked, looking in John's direction.

He looked at Mia for a lingering second and then turned toward me. "Well, I guess the decision before us is to either turn this thing over to the bureau or take it on ourselves. The risk of turning it over to the bureau is that they may not understand what Mia has been through and could place her into custody. But from what you told me last night and what Mia has conveyed this morning, we seem to hold a distinct advantage. With Mia having direct access to the lab and the bottles of H3N7, I'm thinking we formulate a plan to compromise the virus. If you two feel you can continue on your courageous path, I have an idea that might work."

I looked over at Mia, and she was starting to come around. I think she realized that her personal relationship with John was safe and that it was time to reengage.

John continued with his plan. "From what Mia has explained, H3N7 is impervious to heat, chemicals, and most all methods of purification. The only thing that will deteriorate the viral envelope is hydrochloric acid or pepsin. As I understand, it enters the bloodstream and goes straight to the brain. It sustains itself by feeding on the specific proteins found in the thalamus. Mia said there is a small window of time for the virus to make its way to the brain. If you and Mia can gain access to the glass-cleaner bottles holding the virus and add a small amount of hydrochloric acid, it would activate and release the virus. With no proteins available, the virus would starve itself. Is that correct?" John asked Mia.

"That's correct. That small amount of acid would have no effect on the consistency or color of the contents, and the only way they could tell the virus had been compromised would be by viewing it under a microscope. That would take care of the bottles set for distribution, but we must still destroy the parent, H3N7-1. There is only one H3N7-1 strain, and it is kept under lock and key in a safe for reasons of which very few are aware—it is capable of reproduction. It can feed on proteins other than the ones found in the thalamus and does not have the terminal time clock to end its own life. If it were to be released, it would not stop until every living human was destroyed. We must find a way to access H3N7-1 and destroy it," Mia explained.

It was my turn to speak. "My question is, if we managed to compromise the seven bottles and destroy the H3N7, what would stop the demented designers from regrouping and reproducing the virus? I'm sure there are several members with the knowledge and capability to undertake the task."

"I'm afraid that's true, Aubrey," said Mia. "There are five people, including Mark, who can reproduce the H3N7 and the H3N7-1 viruses. Fortunately for us, the five, other than Mark, live here in Atlanta and are not part of the delivery team. We will have to detain them before they realized the plan has been sabotaged."

"As I see this discussion evolve, I'm thinking we should contaminate the seven bottles and let the operation continue as planned," said John. "This will give us a few extra days to decide how to access H3N7-1. The four group members in Atlanta that possess the ability to reproduce the virus will be detained the moment they return to the estate. According to Mia, Mark wants to keep communication silenced during the mission, so we should have no trouble hiding them for a few days. Mia, if this changes, please let me know. As for the members delivering the H3N7, we let them proceed with their mission and capture them as soon as they arrive back in Atlanta. They will have no idea the virus did not activate and will return to the estate expecting to soon hear the news of widespread sickness across the nation. We will apprehend them as they approach the estate's guardhouse and strip them of their cell phones and computers. They will be immediately taken to the safe room," John further explained.

I was starting to feel more comfortable as our plan began to unfold. Mia suggested we take a needed break and meet back in the kitchen in one hour. I climbed the stairs and had entered my room when Mia appeared in the doorway.

She walked over and placed some items on the bed. "Here are some clothes to change into. You're about my size, so help yourself to my closet," she said with a smile.

"Thanks. I already borrowed a pair of someone's Polo pajamas I found in the chest. All I have is the evening gown from last night and maybe a few things in my Jeep. Although the clothes in the Jeep have a distinct odor of *cats*," I said.

Mia rolled her eyes and shook her head. She knew I was never going to forget her sticking me with those nasty cats.

When we met back in the kitchen, I really wanted to switch from coffee to a gin and tonic but did not suggest it. It was probably not the best idea to discuss saving the world under the influence of gin. Everyone looked much better and ready to continue our session.

John spoke first. "We still have to find a way to access the safe and destroy the H3N7 and H3N7-1 viruses. Mia, you have any ideas?"

"Access is only by the imprint of Mark's right hand—well, actually, not just his handprint, but the geometric shape and density of his entire hand. It will be very difficult and complex to try and reproduce. But we could always apply Occam's razor and slice it off and jam it into the safe's portal," Mia said with a hint of amusement in her voice.

Great double entendre, I thought. Just because we had the future of the world in our hands didn't mean we should overlook the opportunity to be clever. I was feeling better as the minutes passed. I liked the plan, and with a few additional details, I believed the three of us sitting at that table might divert a global disaster.

We spent the rest of the day and evening planning and preparing. About eleven thirty, we opened a bottle of Chateau de Seguin

Bordeaux. We poured the entire bottle into three big glasses. Knowing that the day of reckoning was only days away, we enjoyed what would be our last visit over wine until we could hopefully raise our glasses to success.

—

The following day, Mia and I discussed and rehearsed my part of the H3N7 implementation plan. We located the two areas in South and East Atlanta where I would introduce the compromised virus into the city's water system. Both locations were near water treatment plants. Mark had studied and designated locations in each city with the quickest and most direct routes to the waterworks facilities.

On the south side, it was a small restaurant near the sewage treatment ponds. For the life of me, I don't see how anyone could dine with the foul smell of sewage in the air. I opened the car door and was immediately wrapped up in the stench of East Atlanta's morning constitutional. It was horribly disgusting, and I fought not to throw up. I held my breath the best I could and found my way to the ladies' room and confirmed that the water was on and everything was working. I left the restaurant and walked back to the parking lot. As I approached the car, I could see Mia scrolling on her phone with one hand and holding her nose with the other. I was laughing as I jumped back into the car and said, "Let's get out of this stink hole."

The spot in East Atlanta was a bathroom at a MARTA train station. It was a dangerous part of town, and I was glad to have Mia with her service firearm along with me. We didn't exactly fit in and received some threatening looks as we pulled into the parking lot. I told her she could not sit in the car on this one and had to go with me. We walked across the parking lot and down a flight of stairs toward the bathroom. Upon reaching the bottom of the steps, I noticed two of the guys from the parking lot following us. We were alone in the below-ground corridor, and the two men were fast approaching. It was clear they had trouble on their minds and saw us as easy marks.

Mia saw them as well and unbuttoned her overcoat and pulled it to the side, exposing her firearm in a shoulder holster. She casually put her hand on the grip of the gun and started walking the few steps toward them. When she drew her gun, the two men almost lost their pants (literally) as they backpedaled away. They shouted a few expletives while tripping over their sagging pants and attempting to run back up the stairs.

It was scary to think what might have happened if Mia had not been there. I reminded myself to bring my trusty Walther when I returned in a couple of days. We checked out the bathroom and then walked back to the parking lot. The loitering thugs had scattered like roaches and were nowhere to be seen. As we got back to the car, the wind shifted direction and you could smell the telltale signs of sewage. The location was only about a half a mile from another treatment pond.

Mia texted Mark and cryptically informed him that everything had checked out well and that we would meet him and the rest of the group the following evening. He expressed his thanks and told us to be safe and that he would see us the next day.

I thought things were going a little too well. I'm sure I was little paranoid, but who wouldn't be? For all we knew, Mark could be well aware of our betrayal and might be setting a trap. I could envision him meeting us in the deep, dark lab, stories underneath the house, with two body bags waiting and a syringe in his hand.

We ended the day back at Mia's condo. We decided that John needed to be scarce the next few days, and Mia put him on another assignment to keep him occupied. Needless to say, he was not happy.

Although Mark knew about Mia and John's working relationship, he had no idea they had become romantic—or so we assumed. It was best to have John completely out of the picture.

Mia and I broke our no-alcohol rule in less than twenty-four hours. I had gone upstairs to refresh myself, and when I went back downstairs, she was standing in the kitchen with an open bottle of wine and two glasses. "What the hell," she said with a grin.

"What the hell," I replied.

We sat down at the kitchen table and discussed how we would access the glass-cleaner bottles containing the virus. Just then, it occurred to me that this whole secret plan and strategy to curtail the world's destruction had been formulated at a simple Ikea breakfast table in a nondescript condominium. If we could pull this off and save mankind, that little table might join the ranks of the most important tables in the world, like the one where the Declaration of Independence had been signed and the one where the Cabinet gathered at ten Downing Street. It might even be placed in the Smithsonian with wax figures of the three of us! But we still had a few obstacles to overcome before we became world heroes. The first thing we discussed was gaining access to the lab.

Mia felt that we would have no issues with the lab or with introducing the contaminants to the bottles of glass cleaner. She pointed out that, other than Mark, she was probably trusted more than anyone in the group. "I'm their little creation, and I'm sure they have no idea that I turned against them when they decided it was a good idea to kill half the world," she said.

"I see your point, but how can we just waltz into the basement, pull out the syringes, and start stabbing the bottles without anyone noticing? What about cameras, video monitoring, and such?" I asked.

Mia gave me her little smile and said, "Have you forgotten who saved your little ass from the lie detector chair? I'll give you one guess which brilliant person controls the hardware and software for the monitoring system," she said with a smirk.

I raised my glass and gave her a little toast. "You rock."

After a bit more discussion and dining on leftover takeout, we put a wrap on the evening and headed to bed. We would leave for the estate the next morning, and at that point, there would be no turning back. There also would be no contact with John or anyone else. I should have been scared but wasn't. I had become reconciled to the idea that my fate and previous existence had led me to that point; I was there for a reason. I had no idea why such a huge undertaking has been put in my care, but really, why not? There is no rhyme or reason behind the way things happen, and the dynamics of life are a mystery, as they should be.

Chapter Fourteen

We arrived at the estate with little fanfare. The guards ushered us in, and I could sense a little tension in their demeanor. I think they knew something was happening. As we parked, I saw the same line of cars that had been present during my last visit. It appeared that everyone had arrived. I didn't feel nearly as nervous as I had the last time, but the last time I'd had no idea what I was walking into. This time I did. I glanced at Mia, and she gave me one of her little winks. We walked up the driveway and past the garden enclave where my life had been held in balance just a few days earlier. Every day I was more amazed at how life could change directions in a flash. I heeded these thoughts as we approached the door.

We entered the house, and I noticed that none of the servants were present, save the bartender, Walter, who, as I found out during my last visit, was one of us—or should I say one of them? He had already prepared two martinis and handed them to us as we walked into the room. He reported that Mark and the others were in the boardroom anticipating our arrival. I finished the martini in the thirty seconds it took to cross the grand foyer.

As we entered the room, Mark stood and greeted us. "Good evening. Please join us," he said as he pointed to two empty chairs at the end of the table.

After we had taken our seats, I glanced over at Mia, and she knew what I was thinking. She subtly shook her head no, and I took a breath of relief. The last thing I needed was to be wired up to another damn lie detector chair.

"Welcome back. I hope everyone is well rested and prepared for tomorrow's adventure," Mark said as he walked toward the front of the room. "I don't want to be too dramatic, but we've lived most of our adult lives anticipating what is now before us. Countless hours, months, and years have led us to be right here, right now. Fate has delivered us right to the door of the future. Over the next few days, we will fulfill our role with destiny—and nothing can stop us. Dr. Lee embarked on a quest, a vision, and it's our honor to now see it through. Let's raise our glasses and toast Dr. Lee and the history we shall create in a few short hours," he said with the solemn and convincing tone of a motivational speaker.

My martini glass was empty, but I toasted anyway. There was a stir and a rumble as everyone stood and cheered Dr. Lee. The room was charged with excitement, and everyone cheered and applauded as if Dr. Lee were present. I can only imagine what it would have been like if he had actually been there. It was really eerie how everyone was so exuberant about a task that would cause death, destruction, and heartache across the globe. You would think that they were celebrating Dr. Lee being awarded the Nobel Peace Prize. Unfortunately, I think the group viewed what they were doing as having equal or greater status. It was apparent I was in the presence of a high-IQ cult. Fanatics come in all flavors.

I was feeling very uncomfortable, and I'm sure Mia was as well, but we didn't show it. We cheered and clapped like the rest of the zealots. The service, as I would call it, lasted about an hour. It was filled with the same rhetoric that any cult would spout, just on a different topic. Most everyone gave testimonies on the hardships and sacrifices they had experienced over the last twenty years. It became quite emotional at times with people crying and hugging. It reminded me of the churches in the mountains where people handle snakes to prove their dedication to the Holy Spirit.

A spirit was definitely holding power over the room, but it was not holy. It was the spirit of the ultimate serpent, and there was no need for the handling of its subordinates.

After the fervor died down, Mark quickly concluded his talk and wished everyone a pleasant night. We were instructed to meet at seven a.m. in the breakfast room. The vans were departing for the West Coast and the Midwest at 0830.

Mark met Mia and me outside the boardroom and pulled us aside. "Mia, will you do one final inventory and security check on the equipment bags?" he asked.

"Sure, if you think it's necessary, but we secured them last week, and as you know, we're the only ones with keys to the room," Mia replied.

"Yeah, I know, but I just want to check everything one last time. Walter is checking the vans for road worthiness, and they're brand new. You know I obsess over the details. Do you mind?" Mark asked again.

"Not at all; it's a good idea to check behind ourselves. We've come too far for any careless mistakes. Aubrey and I will check the contents and make sure everything is ready. We'll take care of it," Mia said with a confident smile.

"Thank you both," Mark replied with a smile and headed up the spiral staircase.

I could not believe how easy this was turning out to be. I still had my earlier concerns, but if he were going to confront us, I was sure he would have done it by now.

Mia and I met in her room and secured the syringe filled with the hydrochloric acid in her small purse. As we left the room, we engaged in prearranged small talk since there were audio and video cameras every twenty feet along the hallway. The only areas not recorded were the conference room and, supposedly, the bedrooms, basement, and lab. Mark could not take a chance on the signal being intercepted from the outside.

We arrived at the door to the basement, and Mia punched in the code. The door buzzed, then opened, and we descended the stairs and walked down a small hallway. There were several doors located on both sides, and I assumed they marked the entrances to storage closets or other lab rooms. God only knew what was behind the doors, and I was afraid to ask.

We arrived at the end of the hall and entered a large, open laboratory. It was well lit, unlike what I'd imagined, and seemed very sterile and efficient. There were machines running with all kinds of beeps and noises. Different colored liquids were flowing from beaker to beaker. There were no technicians present, and the lab seemed to have a life of its own. It had a menacing feel, like something out of a science fiction novel.

Mia led us to another locked door located on the far side of the room. She repeated the same process used to enter the basement, with an additional step requiring a key to unlock the door. The door opened, and across the room were the seven sinister equipment bags. It was hard to believe that these small everyday, generic bags, capable of holding anything from a kid's lunch to a baby's change of clothes, carried chemicals intended to end millions of lives.

We quickly moved across the room to the bags and located the first bottle of glass cleaner. We carefully took it out of the bag, and I removed the nozzle and held it while Mia operated the syringe. She inserted the allotted amount of acid through the membrane under the cap. I replaced the nozzle and made sure it was in the "off" position, and then returned the bottle to its place and moved on to the next bag. We were on our fifth bag, with our backs to the door, when we heard a stern, confronting voice.

"What are you two doing?"

We froze with the needle inserted into the fifth bottle. Neither of us knew what to do. It appeared we had been set up. I'd known things had been going way too smoothly.

The question came again. "Mia, what are you and Aubrey doing with the bags?"

Mia dropped the syringe into the bag, and we both turned to find Walter standing by the door. She stood up and walked directly to him. "The question is, what are you doing down here? This is off limits to you, and you don't need to know what we're doing. Does Mark know you're down here?" she asked in an aggressive tone.

"No, he doesn't. I was walking down the hall and saw the red light flashing on the security panel, indicating that the basement door was open. I know it's never to be left open and came to check. I'm sorry for startling and questioning you, and you're right—it's not my place to ask what you're doing. Please forgive me," Walter said humbly.

"No problem, Walter. You did the right thing by investigating the open door. I guess we're all a little tense, and I forgot to shut it.

Mark asked me to check the bags one last time, as he asked you to check the vans," Mia said in a softer voice.

Walter apologized again and headed back up the stairs. We heard the door shut, and Mia peeked up the stairs to make sure he was gone.

"Damn, that was close!" I said. "Thank God it wasn't Mark that found the door open and investigated. Do you think Walter is suspicious?"

"No, he has no idea about any of this. I'm fairly certain he didn't see the syringe and wouldn't know what it meant if he did. Let's finish up the last two bags and get the hell out of here."

We finished our task and made our way back upstairs. We walked through the foyer and up the staircase. After a quick hug, we entered our rooms and closed the doors on a very stressful day.

I slipped out of my clothes, got into bed, and pulled the covers as far up as I could. I decided to leave the light on. There was too much darkness in that house, and I could not stand any more. I said my prayers silently and asked for guidance and courage to get through the next day. I prayed that peace would prevail and good would conquer evil. I closed my eyes and drifted off to sleep, knowing and believing that God would only let evil go so far.

—

The vans were to begin rolling at 0830, and there was a nervous excitement in the air. Mark had called in a few of the chefs to prepare breakfast, and it was set out on a buffet in the foyer. It appeared about ten members from the group had shown up to see us off. Everyone was milling around with plates in their hands, talking. I saw who I thought to be the director of the CDC talking to Jason over by the staircase, and they were laughing about something. They had better laugh, I thought; in a few days, there wouldn't be much to find amusing.

Mia and I poured cups of coffee and tried to act jovial along with the rest of the crowd. After breakfast, we all gathered outside and saw the vans were parked by the front door. Mark had brought the equipment bags holding the bottles of glass cleaner up from the basement and had them ready to load. He and Walter put them in the vans, and everything seemed to be going smoothly. The only scenario that worried us was Walter mentioning the syringe to Mark, but, for now, all seemed well.

With everything loaded, the first two vans departed for California on time. Mark was in the first van en route to Los Angeles, and Thomas was in the second, bound for San Francisco. The following four vans departed in fifteen minute intervals. Mia made eye contact with me as she was getting into the passenger seat of the van headed to New York. There was no wink this time; her expression was neutral.

Since my locations were in Atlanta, I would wait seventy-two hours for everyone to be in place. Mark had set the time for 1200 on the third day, and we were all to coordinate around our different time zones.

Before leaving, Mark issued strict instructions on following the rehearsed procedures. None of the group were to have any phone or internet contact with each other. We were expected to make routine phone calls for business and family concerns. "Just another day," as Mark put it. There was an emergency code created to use if a situation arose. The trips would be long ones, and Mark realized he could not control everything.

Mia, John, and I had purchased disposable cell phones a few days earlier. The three of us would stay in contact during the entire operation. We agreed not to use the phones while in public view and would wait until the evening, in the privacy of our rooms, to discuss the day's events.

In exactly seventy-two hours, the contents of the bottles were to be introduced at the two sites in each of the cities. Upon completion, each member would text, "have arrived," signaling that the H3N7 had been dispensed.

What's interesting is that Mark seemed to have little or no concern about me being left alone. Since being introduced to the plan, I haven't been out of sight of at least one of the members. I still don't understand why he involved me, but who am I to second guess a psychopath?

I hung around the estate for a few hours, and it seemed to be business as usual. Today was the staff's last day before what they believed to be a two-week furlough.

With three days to kill, I decided to drive out to Porterdale and check on the RV. It had been several days since I'd left, and I was sure the conditions were deplorable. Before leaving, I'd opened a large bag of cat food and set up three litter boxes. I had no illusions that the cats would not piss and shit on the bed or floor, but I left the boxes anyway. I also cracked a few windows so the cats could come and go. I was hoping they would focus on the "go."

I drove Mia's car back to her condo and retrieved my Jeep. I headed out I-20 East and felt better with every mile I put behind me. As I passed the Conyers exit, things started to feel familiar. Madison and the world I'd left behind were just a few short miles away, and I began to feel anxious. I felt like driving straight back home, burying my head in the sand, and pretending none of this was happening. Of course, I couldn't do that and took the exit for Covington. Before going to Porterdale, I had a little business to tend to.

Being raised in the country, I'm well versed on the value of guns and weapons. Where I come from, they're mostly used for hunting, but country boys do get bored and, for excitement, have been known to take things to another level. Although I had confidence that our plan was sound, my intuition had told me to set up a visit with a resourceful friend in possession of some special supplies.

I pulled into Covington and located my friend's quick lube business for an oil change and tire rotation. The attendant pulled down the garage door as I entered. Thirty minutes later, I left with more than fresh oil and rotated tires.

After arriving in Porterdale, I drove through the quaint mill town and past the Margolin estate. I could not help but think about Alan Margolin. What a horrible tragedy that he'd sent all those boys to a foreign land, afraid and alone, and sold them into slavery. How terrified they must have been when they realized what was taking place. What a miserable life they must have led. My only hope was that they had found peace in a place much better than their earthly home. I also hoped Margolin was paying the wages of sin in a location somewhere far away from the boys.

I turned down Wheat Street just south of town. As I rounded the final curve, I could see the RV was parked just where I'd left it.

"Damn it!" I moaned as I banged my hands on the steering wheel. I was hoping the city had towed it or some desperate soul had stolen the thing. I'd left the door unlocked and the keys in the ignition, but I guess no one had been that desperate. I walked over and hesitantly opened the door. To my dismay, there seemed to be twice the number of cats than I'd left! I guess they'd roamed the hood, putting the word out there was free food and lodging. Anticipating the smell, I pulled out a small bottle of Vicks VapoRub and dabbed a liberal amount under my nose. As strong as the VapoRub was, the horrible smell still assaulted my senses.

After overcoming the stench, I tended to the business at hand. I retrieved a duffle bag and a few larger items from my Jeep and strategically placed them around the RV. I had been given instructions by my friend and followed them to the letter. I then sat behind the wheel of the RV and swiveled the captain's chair around to survey the room. As disgusting as it was, I was trying to convince myself that I needed to stay the night. I'd been told to stick to my cover and follow the plan, but I just didn't think I could do it. Even if I ran all the cats out and shut the windows, the smell would still be intolerable. I decided there was no way in hell I was going to spend that night or any other night in that crap hole. I didn't see why it mattered anyhow. The vans were rolling, the deed was done, and where I spent the night was not going to change anything. I kicked the door shut as I left.

It was getting late, and I drove back to Covington and checked in at the Holiday Inn. As I was unloading my travel bag, I recognized a black Volvo parked in the back of the lot. I'd noticed it several times over the course of the day and figured I was probably being followed. Mark might have turned out to be not as reckless as I'd thought. I'd covered my tracks fairly well and knew that I had not been followed down Wheat Street, and I had kept a keen watch while at the RV. I hoped my precautionary measures would be enough.

After checking in, I walked to my room, looking over my shoulder. I entered and locked all three of the locks on the door. Unbeknownst to Mark, Mia, or John, I possessed the Walther PPK handgun that Colby had loaned me several months before. After moving into an apartment on the edge of shady, I'd felt I needed a little protection. Volvo man was smart to stay in the parking lot.

The next day was uneventful. I stayed in my room, caught up on my sleep, and read the month's book club book, *The Devil in the White City* by Erik Larson. It's a non-fiction book about the events surrounding the 1893 World's Fair, also known as the World's Columbian Exposition. It was strange reading about the country's first serial killer, H.H. Holmes, while trying to stop another one. It was obvious I would be unable to attend our book club meeting and knew they would all be wondering where I was. I could see the club organizer checking his watch and pacing the room. I always liked to be a few minutes late to annoy him. I smiled, thinking about him stressing over my untimely arrival and ultimate absence. It was the only smile I had all day.

Late in the afternoon on the second day in exile, I finally heard from Mia. I was excited to hear from her, which I found kind of strange. She told me that John had set up a meeting tomorrow with their FBI superiors. He had yet to tell them the reason, for fear they would send a surveillance team to track the vans and compromise the operation. As soon as all the "have arrived" messages were received, Mia would inform John, and he would let the cat out of the bag (horrible use of words).

John and Mia had already discussed and devised the intercept plan, and John just needed to review it with the team. At the end of the day, John and Mia would be heroes—or lose their jobs and possibly end up in jail. It was a bold plan and decision, but one made for the love of their country and each other. It was a risk they were willing to take. The alternative was unthinkable.

After talking with Mia, I decided I was becoming a little stir-crazy and ventured down the hall to the lobby. I eased outside for some fresh air and could see from the parking lot lights that the black Volvo was still there. Out of view, I watched for a few minutes and could barely make out the silhouette of someone sitting in the car. I laughed, thinking that the son of a bitch must be more bored than I was, staring out the window, waiting for me to appear. I stopped by the vending machines for a few indulgences and headed back to my room. I secured the locks and settled in for an anxious night of sleep.

I woke the third morning with much anticipation. This was the day that plans would finally be implemented after years of study and preparation. Little did they know that it had only taken a few minutes and a few drops of acid to destroy all their work. My compassionate side felt a little sorry for them, knowing that when they were being led away in handcuffs, they would all realize their hopes and dreams had failed. I quickly snapped out of that train of thought, reminding myself what cold, elitist, sociopaths they were.

—

I left the Holiday Inn and drove back to the estate. The guards waved me through, and I parked in the upper driveway near the entrance to the house. I noticed the Volvo parked just ahead of me. The driver had no idea that I had seen him speed past, attempting to beat me back to the estate. I walked toward the Volvo, and waiting for me was the familiar gatehouse guard. I'd wondered who it would be. He smiled his Andy Griffith grin and, slightly out of breath, welcomed me back. I snickered to myself, watching him massage his neck while talking. We spent a few minutes going over the plan and then left the estate for the locations.

Everything went smoothly as we approached the first drop-off site. The restaurant smelled as foul as it had a few days earlier. I still don't understand how anyone could eat there.

I made my way to the ladies room, locked the door, removed the glass-cleaner bottle from my oversized purse, and poured it down the drain.

As I did, I had a sudden rush of panic, wondering what would happen if the acid had not neutralized the virus. What if Mia really was one of them and had pulled a double or, in this case, a triple cross and had not put the hydrochloric acid in the syringe? A cold sweat engulfed me, and I suddenly felt sick. But it was too late now. If my judgment had been incorrect, I would have the deaths of hundreds of thousands of people on my hands. I splashed my face with cold water and told myself how irrational I was being. Mia and John were just as committed to stopping this madness as I was. I had to collect myself and convince "Andy" all was well.

We drove to the second site, and I repeated the process, except this time I threw a bunch of paper towels into the trash can and poured the contents of the bottles on top of the towels. I'm not sure how safe that was, but it was better than the alternative. If the bottles did contain the virus in an uncompromised form, at least half of Atlanta would be spared. I got back into the van and we drove back to the estate with no conversation. I sent a text to the group: "have arrived."

H3N7, or the compromised version, was making its way to millions of people. The next twenty-four hours would prove to be a relief—or a national catastrophe.

—

After we arrived back at the estate, my guard companion dropped me off at my Jeep and disappeared. He seemed to be in a hurry, probably preparing for what he thought was soon to take place. Hopefully, he would be both surprised and disappointed by the outcome.

I walked to the house. wanting to see if it was really empty. I doubted the house had ever seen a day when there were not at least ten people working. But it was, in fact, empty and seemed more at peace. Maybe even something as inanimate as a house can sense the vibe of evil energy. I took the opportunity to tour the house and admire the amazing architecture and engineering. From the cantilevered spiral staircase to the mosaic ceilings, the house was tremendously impressive. The architect had incorporated the spirit of nature into the plans in a way that was reminiscent of the work of Frank Lloyd Wright. With its organic lines, the mammoth structure seemed to blend in with the surroundings.

I reminded myself that Mark was just passing through this wonderful house and soon would inhabit it no more. He had adulterated the beautiful marble hallways with video and audio monitoring systems. It was an invasion of privacy, and I sensed the eyes of the camera could read my thoughts. The place suddenly felt cold, and it was time to leave.

Mia, John, and I had agreed that I would return to the RV, but now that things were all but over, I decided to head back to Mia's. I drove toward I-20 and made several turns to make sure the guard in the black Volvo was not following me and neither was anyone else.

Upon my arrival, I noticed it was nearing the time for the three of us to have our evening phone call. I opened a bottle of 2007 Stag's Leap, poured a generous glass, and called Mia.

She answered on the first ring. "Aubrey, are you alone?" she asked with a slight note of alarm in her voice.

"Yes, I'm at your condo. What's wrong?"

"Nothing, I think. Let me first say that John's meeting went well with the FBI, and they're fine-tuning our plan to intercept the vans.

But there's been a major change in the plan, and I cannot risk calling John. I need you to call him."

"What changed? Where are you?" I asked.

"I'm at JFK, getting ready to board a plane back to Atlanta. Mark informed us a few hours ago that everyone is flying back to Atlanta and will be at the estate by late evening."

"Shit! Do you think he suspects something?"

"No. He's always paranoid and famous for changing things at the last minute. He probably planned on us taking flights home from the start. The problem is that John and the units are planning on mobilizing tomorrow morning for the intercept, and by that time, we'll all be back at the estate. You have to call him and tell him about the change. I'm about to board and will miss our evening call."

I immediately called John and broke the news to him.

"This is bad; I've got to run and figure out a new intercept plan. Will call soon," John replied and abruptly disconnected.

Events were moving, directions were changing, and I was not surprised. As I sat at the future Smithsonian table, I did not feel as confident without Mia and John. We'd sought to divide our enemies, but it seemed we were the ones being divided at that point. Things were getting complicated, and the three of us were scattered and unable to collectively communicate. I called Mia back and left her a message that John was aware and working on a new plan. I wished her a safe passage and headed up the stairs to bed.

—

After a restless night, I awoke to the singing of birds. I could hear them just outside my window and listened to their inspiring melody. I had no illusions that the day would stay peaceful and bright, but I didn't let that spoil my temporary enjoyment. After a few minutes, I

pulled myself out of bed and prepared for the uncertainty of the day. I
lingered a little longer at the condo and reluctantly left for the estate.

After a quick stop by Starbucks to get the strongest coffee available, I approached Paces Ferry Road with moisture on my hands. I
held the steering wheel tightly, and my stomach felt like a swarm of
bees. I had to calm and collect myself for whatever I would find at
the estate. Neither Mia nor John had called that morning, so I had
no idea what I would encounter.

I pulled down the drive and past the gatehouse. I walked past
the garden, and approached the house. As I reached for the door, it
was suddenly opened from the inside. Someone quickly grabbed me
and pulled me into the house. I was startled, and it took me a second
to react. The entire foyer was filled with people who I assumed were
FBI agents. The flights would have arrived late the previous night, so
I guess it had made sense to intercept the group at the estate.

"Come on over, Aubrey; you're the last of the group to arrive,"
John said in a tone of indifference as he motioned me to join him
across the room. I took immediate notice that he referred to me as
one of the group, and I did not appreciate the reference. Mia stood
a few feet behind him, talking to a fellow agent. I then noticed that
four members of the group were sitting on a Victorian bench against
the spiral staircase. They all had their hands zip tied behind their
backs and their heads lowered. You could see their feelings of defeat.
Mia and I made five and six, and you can guess who was missing. I
made my way across the room and joined John.

"Well, I'm sorry I'm late. Do you want me to go join the others?"
I asked with a little irritation and attitude as I pointed over toward
the Victorian bench. John took a deep breath and realized he had
been out of line.

"I'm sorry, Aubrey. I didn't mean to be short or imply you were one of them. It's been a long and stressful night. Please forgive me."

I told him he was forgiven as Mia walked up and gave me a big hug. "God, it's good to see you. I'm so glad this is almost over," she said.

I knew what she meant by "almost over," and I asked the question. "Where's Mark?"

With a tired look, she just shrugged her shoulders. "No one knows. He wasn't on any of the flights from Los Angeles."

As Mia was talking, the front door opened. We all turned to see who it was. Of course, we were hoping it was Mark with his hands cuffed behind his back. It was not Mark, but a young house servant being escorted by an agent. It was a scene that did not fit. We all just stood there for a moment trying to figure out why she was there.

John asked the question that was on all our minds. "What are you doing here?" he asked the young woman directly.

"I don't know. I guess coming to work?" she replied.

"Who told you to report to work?" he asked.

"Mr. McClure, of course," she answered with a confused look. You could have heard the proverbial pin drop in the midst of the silence. Everyone, including the captives, focused on the maid.

Mia, recognizing her, walked over and spoke. "You're Claire, aren't you?"

"Yes, Ms. Mia. What's going on?" she asked, frightened.

"Everything's fine. We just want to ask you a few questions. Do you mind?"

"No, of course not. Am I in trouble?" the girl asked.

"No, not at all. We were just wondering why Mr. McClure asked you to come in today," Mia calmly explained.

"I don't know. He's called several times the past couple of days to check on me," Claire responded.

"Why would he need to check on you?" Mia asked.

"I'm not sure, but it might have something to do with the morning you all left in the vans."

This got everyone's attention, and we all moved in close to listen. I looked back at the group, and they were all leaning forward on the bench, straining to hear what she was about to say.

"What happened?" Mia asked. Claire looked very uncomfortable with everyone watching her. She also seemed reluctant to speak.

"It's okay, Claire. We really need to know exactly what happened that morning," Mia said in a gentle tone.

"Well, I was in the front hallway cleaning the big mirror when Mr. McClure passed me, headed toward the front entrance. I said, 'Good morning,' but he didn't respond. Then, after a few steps, he stopped and walked back to where I was working. He just stared at me for a couple of seconds, and I asked him if I could be of any assistance. I felt nervous and just stood there waiting."

The young girl took a pause, and Mia coaxed her to continue. "Very good, Claire; you're doing great. What happened next?"

"He pointed to the mirror and said it had not been cleaned properly. I had just cleaned it, and it was spotless. I didn't know what to say. I told him I would clean it again immediately. He said never mind, that he would do it himself. He pulled a bottle of glass cleaner from a bag he was carrying and began to spray the mirror. Instead of spraying the mirror, he accidentally sprayed me. I inhaled the cleaner and started coughing and had to sit down. I guess he was embarrassed, because he quickly turned away and left the hallway."

We knew where this story was going.

"Claire, tell me exactly what has happened since then, up until now, involving any conversation or contact with Mr. McClure," Mia said, the stress coming through in her voice.

The girl did not hesitate with her answers. She knew something important was happening. "The next day, Mr. McClure called to ask how I was. I think he was concerned about me breathing in the ammonia from the cleaner."

"This is very important, Claire. What exactly did you tell him?"

We were all holding our breath, waiting on her answer.

"Well, I didn't answer the phone. Being that we were off for the next couple of weeks, I'd had a little too much to drink the night before and was not feeling well. My brother answered the phone and told Mr. McClure I was sick and could not come to the phone."

You could hear a collective sigh from the room, but it did not last for long.

"But he called yesterday morning, and I told him I was feeling much better and looking forward to coming back to work. He asked if I could come in first thing this morning. He said he wanted me to deliver a message . . . but never told me what it was."

Chapter Fifteen

Time froze in that moment, and when it began again, things were immediately frantic!

Without a word, Mia and John ran toward the back of the house. The captives, desperate to escape, had fallen off the bench and were twisting and turning on the floor, trying to save themselves. To me, the frenzy appeared to unfold in slow motion, like a violent car crash.

I never moved an inch. Everything seemed surreal, and I found myself caught up in the rhythm of all that was happening. I could hear every scream, cry, and hopeless plea and felt the panic around me, which came mostly from the captured conspirators. There was one low sound that stood out from the rest, and I could just hear it over the hysteria. It was a consistent, familiar sound, but I could not immediately identify it.

I froze with fright when I realized what it was and what it meant. I have no idea how I knew what was about to happen—I just did. I also knew at that moment that he had beaten us.

Running outside, I saw a large, black helicopter hovering about a thousand feet over the house. I immediately knew who was in the helicopter and that we only had seconds to live. I flashed back to my track days and ran as fast as I could away from the house. Just as I got to the small driveway garden, I heard and felt the explosion. It lifted me about ten feet into the air and propelled me another twenty. I could feel the heat of the blast, and it felt like my body was on fire. I'm not sure how long I flew through the air, but it felt like a lifetime as I waited to crash back to the ground and certain death.

To my surprise, in a fluke that I can only attribute to fate, I landed in the middle of the large koi pond just off the garden enclave. Lying on my back and under two feet of water, I could not hear, feel, or sense anything from the outside world. It was a temporary refuge from the hell happening just feet away. As I lay under the water, my overloaded, stressed mind began to fill with hallucinations. I could see a baby grand piano floating in the air above me. *What an odd place for a piano*, I thought. I started playing in my mind the theme to *Ice Castles*, the only tune I knew. Suddenly, the piano was much closer, and I realized what was happening. I sprung out of the pond like a new convert seconds before the piano crashed down in the spot I had just been occupying.

Out of the water and back into the world, I could feel the ground shaking and hear the horrible sound of more explosions. Before I could move, I was immediately knocked down by a piece of the flying piano. It hit me square between my shoulders and sent me rolling. I was quickly back on my feet and moving fast toward a nearby line of trees. I jumped behind a layer of dense brush and took a second to see if anything was broken or bleeding. I had what felt like an intense sunburn, but everything seemed to move like it should, and I could not see any blood.

It was then that I looked back at the estate, expecting to see people running and shouting, the wounded being attended to, and just general chaos, but it was not there. It was simply gone. There was no burning shell or fragmented foundation; it had just ceased to exist. The surrounding landscape was littered with parts of the house and its contents.

With horror, I thought about Mia, John, the young maid, and even the handcuffed captives. Everything had disappeared in less than two minutes. As reality began to set in, I heard it again—the low, soft thuds of rotor blades changing pitch as the helicopter banked away from the devastation.

My first thought was, *God damn Mark McClure.* Until then, I had never seen nor did I realize there could be so much evil in a person. My thought was not a slur against God; it was a plea.

I looked toward the parking area and saw that the cars were in disarray and that a few were on fire. I worked my way through the rubble and found that my Jeep was still on four wheels. It had a car leaning on two wheels against it, but it seemed intact. I jumped in, held my breath, and turned the key. It started and I put it in forward gear and mashed the accelerator. With a loud groan of angry metal, it lurched from its spot as the leaning car crashed into the space. The driveway was mostly clear, having been protected by a stand of oak trees that took the brunt of the explosion. I still had to maneuver over and around small piles of debris but made it to the main road.

To my disbelief, parts of the house were littered all over Paces Ferry Road and had caused considerable carnage. People injured and possibly dead were lying in the middle and on the side of the road.

Cars were upside down and on fire. It all looked like a scene from a war-torn country. I could hear emergency vehicles in the distance, but they were unable to get to the scene. There was no way to turn in either direction onto Paces Ferry, but I was not going to remain in the vortex of that hell any longer.

I drove the Jeep straight across the road, through a two-foot drainage ditch, and into a parking lot. I could see that a side road accessed the lot near the rear, and I raced across the lot toward the exit. I turned west onto the road, not knowing or caring where it led. As I sped away from the black, billowing smoke of the doomed estate, I realized that everything had changed again. Change seemed to be the only constant in my life, and I was overdue for a positive one. Reviewing my current circumstances, I knew that was not in my immediate future, and my sole focus was survival. I worked my way back to I-20 and drove east, away from Atlanta.

My first thought after I'd had time to take a breath was that Mia and John were gone and I was all alone. I wasn't sure if Mark had seen me escape or thought I was dead like all the others, but I was not going to take a chance and return to Madison. Porterdale and the RV seemed like the safest place to go and that safety would probably not last for long.

On the interstate, I kept an eye in the rearview mirror, half expecting to see the Volvo. Every car looked suspicious, and any of them could have been carrying an assassin. With my reckless departure, I certainly would have drawn the attention of anyone watching the estate. I grabbed the handgun from my purse and stuck it under my leg. The Walther PPK might have given me a false sense of security, but it made me feel safe nonetheless.

I was trying desperately not to think about Mia and John, but my heart was too heavy and I felt the tears running down my face.

All they had wanted was an opportunity to love each other. There had been so much adversity surrounding their lives and all odds had been against them, but their love had been too strong to be overcome. It saddened and frightened me how the darkness of evil had so quickly extinguished the light of love. I couldn't stop crying, knowing their beautiful love story was over forever. It made everything seem hopeless.

I reached the Covington exit and dried my eyes. As devastated as I felt, I knew I had to be strong. With Mark still out there, this was far from over. I pulled into Covington and looked for a grocery store to stock up on supplies. I chose Walmart because even as bad as I looked, I knew I would not stand out among that crowd. I grabbed food, water, and a couple of bottles of wine before leaving the store for Porterdale.

It was just before noon, and I was not ready to face the RV or the cats. My emotions were shot, and the only thing that made sense was to temporarily numb myself and get drunk. I stopped off at the familiar Jimbo's and made my way to the bar. The place held a lot of recent memories. My first visit had been with Colby after a shoe-shopping trip to Conyers. We'd stopped on our way back to Madison and had a great afternoon talking and sipping wine. The last was the ill-fated day I met Mark for lunch and was pulled further into this madness.

After my third beer, I could feel my body start to relax, and I began to enjoy the effects of the alcohol. There was no one else at the bar, and for just a second, I was able to detach myself from everything—until I made the mistake of glancing up at the TV. The banner at the bottom of the page read, "Breaking News." A camera from a helicopter panned over the fire and destruction at the doomed estate. It would have been shocking to see, even if I had not been there to experience it.

I asked the bartender to turn up the volume. We both watched as the live report continued: "At least a dozen bodies have been discovered after an early-morning explosion at a Buckhead estate. Officials are reporting that at approximately nine o'clock a.m., a huge explosion leveled the large estate home and caused casualties within the estate and on the neighboring Paces Ferry Road. It's unknown what caused the explosion, and the FBI has officially taken over the investigation. We've yet to learn the name of the estate's owner but hope to have it for you shortly. We will remain live on the scene and provide you with minute-by-minute updates . . ."

I laid a twenty on the bar and left before I became sick. The TV report had confirmed the reality of the situation. There was no way to escape it. I made it back to my car as the horror of it all came crashing down. I crawled into the back seat and began crying and shaking uncontrollably. I'd never felt so desperate and alone in my life.

I'm not sure how long I slept, but when I opened my eyes, it was dark. I was disoriented, and it took a few seconds to figure out where I was. I climbed into the front seat and could feel the chill of the night air. I started the engine and waited for the heat. I was shaking and my teeth were chattering, partly from fear but mostly from the cold. As I waited to warm up, I thought about my options, and the RV unfortunately still seemed to make the most sense. Mark was aware of it, I was sure, but I was banking on him believing I was among the dead.

I left Jimbo's parking lot and drove the two miles to the RV. As I passed the Margolin estate, I involuntarily thrust the middle finger of my left hand in its direction. It was definitely not one of my most stable emotional moments! I pulled up to the RV, and everything was dark.

I was terribly scared and gripped the Walther tightly. Very quietly, I opened the truck door, and the darkness was immediately penetrated by every damn light in the Jeep. Surely there must be a way to turn the damn things off! If anyone was watching, they certainly knew I was there and alone. I grabbed the flashlight from the glove box with minimal expectations. To my surprise, it turned on and shot out a four-foot beam. I held the gun close to my chest and the flashlight low and to my side.

I approached the RV with much dread and held my breath. I reached for the door handle and slowly turned it. I had only pulled it open a few inches when it slammed against me, hitting my arm and knocking the gun from my hand.

I could feel the presence of something rushing me. I closed my eyes, knowing there was nowhere to run and nothing I could do. I just wanted it to end quickly, but nothing happened. I opened my eyes to see two big tomcats running past me, chasing a few smaller cats.

"Motherfucker!" was my first reaction, and my second was to pick up the gun and shoot them. Fortunately for them, they did not stick around and ran into the darkness. I took a deep breath and entered the motor home. Having lost the element of surprise, I turned on all the lights. There were about six cats stirring around the table, and I threatened them with a convenient can of Lysol. They let out hisses and headed out the window.

I moved to the rear of the RV and removed the tape sealing the bedroom door. The smell in that room was not so bad, but I sprayed another few shots of Lysol to get me through the night. I shut and locked the door and collapsed onto the bed. Since the room was freezing and I was totally exhausted, I climbed under the covers fully clothed. I still had my trusty Walther clutched in my right hand and stuck it under the pillow. I felt a little apprehensive about falling asleep, but I was fading fast. My last thoughts were dark visions about what the next day might bring. The words from a Doris Day song entered my mind and I softly began singing "Que Sera, Sera."

Whatever will be, will be, I thought.

—

Later, a slight vibration of the worn-out RV woke me from a light sleep, and I knew the disturbance was too heavy to have been caused by the cats.

I had barely processed the thought when my door came crashing open. I quickly tried to pull the Walther from under the pillow, but I was too late. One of the intruders was on top of me before I could react. A second one grabbed my legs, and I could not kick free. I could feel claustrophobia take over as I was being pinned down, and I could not move.

It appeared my fate was again in the hands of Mark.

"He said not to kill her. He wants her alive, but *barely alive* was his instruction," the guy holding my legs said.

"Maybe we could have a little fun with her before we take her back. He's going to kill her anyway," the intruder on top of me said.

I could see this going from bad to worse.

"Let's take her clothes off and see what we got. How about it, little lady? You got something for us?" one of them said.

As he moved off of me, I gave no resistance, and he let go of my arms, which he had pinned behind my head. I slipped my arm under the pillow and removed the gun and slid it down by my side. He then pulled back the cover with an evil look, which quickly turned to surprise. Before he could get a word out or move, I raised the Walther and shot him twice. The second guy was directly behind him and caught one of the bullets. They both hit the floor like sacks of shit.

I let out a deep breath and lowered the Walther to my lap. That turned out to be a big mistake. They were both back on me in seconds. It appeared my shots had been left of center and destroyed the first guy's left jaw. One of the bullets had hit the second guy in the neck. Both had blood pouring out of them, and they were not about to let me have another shot.

I felt the hard steel of the gun connect with the top of my head. I was instantly shaken and could see bright, shooting lights pass through my vision. The Walther scattered to the floor as the second blow hit the side of my head. As I waited for the final blow, I realized that they were no longer planning on taking me alive. I could sense the motion as the guy drew back to crash the gun into my head again.

Suddenly, the whole RV lit up with bright, flashing lights. I could feel no pain and was momentarily confused. I then heard a horn blowing in conjunction with the lights. The intruders disappeared as fast as they had appeared. I am sure Mark told them that getting caught was not an option. I wondered who had pulled up, and that was my last thought as the room began to spin and everything faded to black.

Chapter Sixteen

Colby

"So Colby was the person pulling up to the RV?" Nathan asked.

"Yeah, and had he not arrived at that moment, I would have never made it out of there alive," Aubrey said softly.

Both of them looked over my way, and we were all silent. The last twenty-four hours had been a blur, driven by reaction and the need to survive. Sitting at the table, listening to Aubrey describe the final details, I realized how brave and courageous she had been. I could see the enormity of the situation along with the loss of her friends reflected in her tired, defeated eyes. She had dodged death several times in the last several days and knew she would probably need to do it again soon.

It had been a long, exhausting day. Aubrey told her story in short episodes in between her painful headaches and frequent naps. As the day came to a close, it became apparent that more troubled times lay ahead. I suggested we open a bottle of wine and go watch the sunset from the side porch. Aubrey sat in a large Adirondack chair with her legs pulled to her chest. Despite the peaceful setting, we were all out of words as we watched the swirls of color paint the sky.

I headed to the kitchen and prepared a platter of summer sausage, Gouda cheese, jalapeno jelly, and bagel chips. It was not much of a meal, but I don't think any of us had much of an appetite. I took the platter out to the deck, and we ate in silence, staring off toward the fading sunset.

"I think we should finish up and call it a day," Nathan said.

"I agree," I answered.

Aubrey just nodded.

We walked back inside the house and said goodnight. Aubrey and Nathan went to their bedrooms, and I cleaned up and fed the dogs. They wagged their tails, accepting the food, and were oblivious to any of our concerns.

I locked the doors and noticed the moon was a full hunger moon. The Creek and Cherokee Indians described the winter moon as a hunger moon, depicting harsh, tough conditions. That was certainly an apt description for our situation.

I turned off the lights and headed for my bedroom. I was lying there, trying to make sense of things and wondering what the next day would bring, when I heard a small tap at my door.

"Come in," I said quietly.

It was Aubrey, and she was crying.

"Do you mind if I sleep in here tonight?" she asked gently, barely able to speak. I got up and helped her to bed. I could feel her fear ebb as I wrapped my arms around her. Even the strongest of people sometimes needed to be held.

—

Later, I was startled awake by the sound of Hannah and Savannah launching from the front porch. I could hear their claws digging into the wood as one let out a startling bark—a bark I knew very well. I sat up straight in bed, alarmed. The light on my laptop was fiercely blinking red. There was supposed to be an audible alarm as well, but it didn't go off. I can only assume I'd muted it at some point, a potentially fatal mistake.

I leaned over and shook Aubrey. "Get up and get dressed," I told her. "They've found us!"

She hit the floor and grabbed her clothes. I could see the curve of her body in the wash of the moonlight. In the midst of all that was happening, I had to pause for a split second and take her in. The sight instantly reminded me of late summer nights on the dock by the river. We would go for a swim, and the moonlight would reflect on her as she climbed the ladder to retrieve her clothes. Her profile had not changed a bit.

I hurriedly threw on my jeans, shirt, and boots and ran from the room to get Nathan. He met me in the hallway already dressed and alert. I guess all those nights in Vietnam, sleeping in drainage ditches under a poncho, had trained and prepared him for situations like this.

I had them come with me quickly into a walk-in closet in my bedroom. I opened the large gun safe and handed rifles to Nathan and Aubrey, a DPMS .223 and an AR-15. Both were loaded with extended, fifty-round magazines. I grabbed my Saiga 410 semiautomatic shotgun that was housed with a drum containing thirty 410 slugs.

We ran to the window and cautiously looked out. The dogs had retreated to the porch and were barking like hell. We could not see anything, but I knew they were close. I glanced over at Nathan and saw the look of alarm on his face. I knew he was thinking we should get moving before we got trapped in the house.

He was right, and I took immediate action. Normally I would have prefaced my next comments with something clever, but I just said, "Watch this." I grabbed my laptop, moved the cursor to an icon, and clicked. The sky lit up like Armageddon.

I had previously installed blast-proof windows, so we were protected, but my heart sank as I wondered how the dogs had fared in the explosion.

It was now time to move. We ran down to the end of the hall, where I quickly opened a closet used for linens. I dragged all the sheets and towels into the hallway. I grabbed the shelving racks and tossed them out as well. The others stood there looking at me like I had lost my mind. I pressed a button on the inside of the door frame and a hatch opened, revealing a tight, three-step stairwell leading to two tunnels. The tunnels were about three feet high and three feet wide. The one on the right was approximately seventy-five feet long and terminated into a large doghouse behind my woodshed. The tunnel would be cramped and claustrophobic, but it would serve the purpose of getting us out of the house undetected. If we made it out of there that night, I knew I would have a lot of explaining to do.

We crawled single file through the dark, dirt tunnel. Holding a small flashlight, Nathan led the way with Aubrey in the middle and me bringing up the rear with the weapons. I could hear Aubrey gasping for breath and told her to hang on. After a couple of minutes, we reached the end of the tunnel, and I instructed Nathan to raise the false bottom inside the doghouse. I had it mounted on a hydraulic hinge, and it quietly opened into the night sky.

We quickly exited, and I handed the weapons to Nathan and Aubrey. I could hear the sounds of the wounded and could smell the cordite in the air. I was hoping the explosions at the front of the house had caused enough confusion to divert their attention from our whereabouts. We moved into the woods with the cover of the trees and continued our escape.

There was an old roadbed not far from the house that was overgrown and not visible. I had purposely let the weeds grow but kept a path just wide enough for an ATV. It was about a mile long and ended near an abandoned and forgotten kaolin mine.

This was to be our escape route. While Nathan and Aubrey had slept the morning before, I had parked a Polaris 850cc ATV at the entrance to the old road. You can imagine that someone who placed explosives around the perimeter of his house and had dug an escape tunnel would have a vehicle ready for an immediate departure. I'd gotten the idea from the book *Patriots* by James Wesley Rawles.

The distance from the doghouse to the ATV was, unfortunately, about forty yards. The woods would have normally served as adequate cover, but we were at a disadvantage with the bright moonlight. We decided to make a run for the ATV but had only made it about ten yards when we heard yelling and then gunfire. With the aid of the full moon and probably infrared night-vision goggles, they had found us.

We hit the ground and took cover behind a large oak tree. It had been a recent victim of violent summer storms and now protected us from the hail of bullets.

Saving us now was beyond the scope of my abilities. I looked at Nathan, and he understood my silent message.

"Follow my instructions and do not hesitate," he ordered. "Move low and fast toward the ATV with me behind you providing firing cover. Move in ten-yard intervals, then drop and provide cover for me. Count your steps so you will stop at the same point. I will move to your left, and you will fire straight ahead. When I arrive, already be moving toward the next position and repeat. Remember, you only have fifty rounds, so shoot in short, three-to-five-round bursts. When

I start firing, you two run like hell. Colby, give me the Saiga, and you take the rifle." It only took about ten seconds for him to instruct us. It was evident that he had given similar instructions before. "Do you both understand?" he quickly asked.

We both signaled that we did.

"Go now!" Nathan yelled as he fired in the direction of our assailants.

We followed Nathan's plan of retreat, and it worked as if we had practiced it a hundred times. We made it to the ATV just as we were firing the last rounds of ammo. I'd positioned the ATV behind a large pile of sand, next to the old roadbed. The assailants were getting close and firing into the sand pile.

"Colby, that's all I got. You need to take it from here," Nathan said, breathing heavily and leaning against the ATV.

I pulled out my iPhone and slid it to life. Aubrey and Nathan looked at me with surprise. I knew what they were thinking: *Surely he doesn't believe he has time to call for help!*

For the second time in less than fifteen minutes, I said, "Watch this." They did not need to be told to hold their ears and hit the deck. I touched an app with an icon shaped like a stick of dynamite, and once again, within seconds, the sky lit up and the ground shook. The blast gave us enough time to mount the ATV and continue our escape.

I was familiar with the path and, with the assistance of the moonlight, didn't need the ATV's headlamp. We drove through the darkness for about ten minutes and arrived at the old kaolin mine. I wasn't sure what to do next. In hindsight, I should have left a vehicle at the end of the road, but I hadn't planned that far ahead and hoped it would not cost us. Both Aubrey and Nathan looked at me as if to ask, "What now?"

We were in my part of the world, and it was my responsibility to get us to safety. A flicker of a plan started to take shape.

"The airport is about seven miles from here. This dirt road leads to Mt. Zion Road, which intersects the Linton Road, and then to the airport. The roads are dirt the entire way except for the last two or three miles. I think we can easily make it on the ATV." They both knew where I was headed.

"So you're thinking we make our escape in your airplane?" Aubrey asked.

"That's the best plan I can think of. I suppose we could try to make it back to town and alert the police, but we would have to travel the major roads, and I'm sure Mark's men are patrolling them. Only locals know these dirt roads, and I'm betting they've not factored in an escape by air."

Nathan jumped back on the ATV and said, "Sounds like our best option is the airplane. Let's get moving."

With me driving, Aubrey in the middle, and Nathan in the rear, perched on a small patch of seat, we followed the roads to the airport. The constant drone of the rubber tires on the road was hypnotizing. No one said a word on the twenty-minute ride; we just huddled together tightly as a unit.

The adventures of the last several days had built a bond of reliance and trust. One never knows who one can count on until one's survival is in the hands of another person. I could say without any doubt that I could count on those two. We were like a band of brothers (and sister). Well, I guess after the night before, the term "sister" might not be appropriate.

Approaching the airport, I could see the rotating beacon flashing white, then green. For many years that beacon had been a welcoming site, guiding me along the final distance to the airfield, and that night would be no different. We arrived at the airport and eased our way over to my hangar. All seemed still and quiet. I did not have my key but had one hidden under a concrete block a few feet from the door. I opened the door and turned on the lights. N7571Q was there waiting for me like an old friend. I had saved the airplane after it had been neglected and abandoned at an airport near Aiken, South Carolina. It took two years, but I had restored the Cessna 182P back to its original condition.

I pressed the button that opened the large hangar door, and then we pushed 71Q out of the hangar and aligned it with the taxiway. I instructed my two passengers to get in and buckle up. I pointed to two headsets and told them to put them on. After doing a quick walk around the exterior, I joined them in the airplane. I pulled out my checklist and quickly ran through all the pre-flight requirements. The fuel tanks had been filled after the previous flight, so fuel was not an issue. Everything checked out fine, and the last thing to confirm was that the rotating beacon and strobe light were working properly. I leaned out my door and looked toward the back. I could see the moonlight reflecting on the fuselage and vertical stabilizer. It was the second time that night I had admired the beauty of a profiled figure.

Out of habit, I cleared the prop (announcing to anyone outside of the airplane that the propeller is about to spin) and then started the engine. Oil pressure shot straight to the green, and all the gyros spun up properly. I usually do a complete engine and system run-up, but that night would be the exception. I checked to see that my passengers were strapped in and had radio intercom communication. They each gave me a thumbs up, and we taxied to runway 31 in radio silence. As I neared the end of the southeast taxiway, I clicked my microphone three times on frequency 123.0. The runway lights appeared and lit up like two bands of pearls, outlining our route to escape.

I centered the Cessna on the runway and applied full power. The noise was loud, and the cockpit lights gave out an amber glow. At about a thousand feet down the runway, I pulled back on the yoke, and eager to leave land, the airplane jumped for the sky. We climbed at fifteen hundred feet per minute and leveled out at five thousand feet. I set the propeller and RPMs for cruise speed and engaged the autopilot. I keyed the mic and said, "It may not last long, but for now, our troubles are far below us."

After few minutes of flying the runway heading, it was time to decide on a direction. I asked if anyone had any ideas.

Nathan spoke up and said, "Fly a heading of 270."

Having flown that heading, or direction, many times, I knew it would take us straight back toward Atlanta. I had no idea what he was thinking but turned the airplane to 270 degrees and began a turn to the course heading.

—

The full moon lit up the sky, and the horizon was endless. It is mysteriously beautiful to fly at night and see all the lights below. I imagined people sitting on their porches hearing the lone sound of the airplane's engine and wondering where I was going, maybe dreaming it was them flying off to an unknown destination. To escape and be separated from the earth is good for the soul. Unfortunately, with only four hours of fuel on board, we would eventually have to return to earth and face the troubles awaiting us.

We flew west toward Atlanta and were quickly approaching class B airspace. To enter class Bravo airspace, a twenty-mile vertically layered perimeter around the Atlanta airport, you must be on an approved flight plan or have gained permission from air traffic control. Also, your aircraft must be equipped with a mode C transponder. The transponder allows ATC to track your position and provide collision avoidance. Normally, I would have contacted Atlanta approach, given them my aircraft tail number, and enlisted radar service, but with smart phone applications able to track active flights, it was not an option. I knew it would not be long before our trackers discovered our escape by air and would use all methods to find us. Without radar service, I would have to keep a sharp eye out for traffic, but it was worth the risk of not giving up our position.

I could see the lights of Covington on the horizon, which was located right on the edge of the Bravo airspace. We were currently over Madison, but I did not mention it to Aubrey or Nathan. None of us needed to be thinking about home. As we approached Bravo airspace, which is the airspace around major cities and airports that pilots are not allowed to enter without permission from air traffic control, we had to make a decision. Since we were not in mode C and in radio silence, our choices were limited to non-controlled airports. There are several on the outskirts of the city, but they're difficult to get into at night without guidance. It was time to find out why Nathan had chosen west.

"Nathan, what's your strategy on flying toward Atlanta?" I asked.

"I have a feeling Mark's in the Atlanta area, and I think I know where he is," Nathan replied.

His answer got our attention, and we both asked, "Where?" at the same time.

"If your family of twenty years is dead, or in the hands of the authorities, and your home and refuge no longer exist, where would you go?"

Aubrey and I weren't in the mood for riddles, but I could see where he was headed. He wanted us to think like Mark. It took a few seconds, but then it made complete sense.

"Dr. Lee's," I answered.

"You are correct," he replied.

"Aubrey, you mentioned Mia said her dad still lived in the Atlanta area. Do you remember where?"

"Ahhh... Let me think. I do remember her telling me he retired near Atlanta, but I don't remember where."

About a minute went by, and I was beginning to make a turn away from the Bravo airspace when Aubrey broke the silence. "Braselton. He moved to a small farm in Braselton!" she said with excitement in her voice.

"Colby, is there an airport in Braselton?" Nathan asked.

"No, but there are several nearby, Gainesville being the closest, but it's controlled, and to land we would have to communicate. Winder is only about twenty or so miles from Braselton and is uncontrolled. Actually, it's very similar to Sandersville with runways 31/13. If you're thinking what I think you are, the Barrow County Airport would be our best option," I answered.

"I can't speak for either of you, but I don't take too well to being hunted," said Nathan. "I think it's time we do the hunting. Do you both agree?"

I saw Aubrey put her hand on Nathan's shoulder and give an affirmative nod. He looked over at me, and I nodded as well.

"Colby, take us to Winder." Nathan instructed.

I had no idea what his plan was, but I had total confidence in Nathan. I disengaged the autopilot and made a right turn to a heading of forty-five degrees. I entered KWDR (the identifier for the Winder airport) into the GPS and pushed the navigate button. It locked on forty-seven degrees and reported thirty-nine miles and an ETA of seventeen minutes. I reengaged the autopilot and began studying the landing information. I monitored the UNICOM frequency 122.8

and did not hear any communication around the airport. I decided to go in silently and draw as little attention as possible.

At three miles out, headed for a straight-in landing on runway 31, I began my pre-landing checklist. I adjusted my airspeed and power settings and began to lower the flaps, which assisted in slowing down the airplane. I then clicked the microphone button three times, and the runway appeared out of the darkness. As most rural airports, the radio frequency at the airfield is pilot activated. I followed the visual approach slope indicator, and our descent was right on course. At the last second, I turned on the landing light and, with three chirps from the tires, we were back on the ground.

I taxied to the ramp, past a long line of airplanes. I shut down the engine and avionics, and the only sound was the whining of the gyros winding down.

I looked over at Nathan and said, "You're in charge, boss."

He stuck out his hand and asked "May I borrow your cell phone?"

—

We exited the airplane and secured it with the tie-downs located on the ramp. The moon was high off the horizon, and I noticed it now was encompassed by a lunar halo. Over the centuries, there have been many hypotheses on what a lunar halo signifies. The farmers believe it meant bad weather, and others believed it was a symbol of bad things to come—I was going with the bad weather.

A quick survey of the airfield indicated that we were alone. As we walked toward the Fixed Base Operation, also known as the terminal, Nathan asked me to be ready with a pen and paper. I wondered what he had in mind. The last few days had been full of surprises, and I was sure that was not about to change. We reached the door to the Fixed Base Operation, and Nathan turned the handle to find it was locked. "Damn!" he said. "It looks like we'll have to find another way in."

"1228," I said. They both gave me a puzzled look. "Punch the UNICOM frequency 1228 into the keypad beside the door," I said and pointed to the keypad. Nathan entered the code, and the door made a clicking sound and unlatched.

"Some of that pilot shit, I presume," Nathan said with a grin.

We entered the FBO, and the glow of the computer monitor pointed our way to the pilots' lounge. We sat at the table, and Nathan pulled out my phone and made a call. It took about ten seconds, and it appeared someone had answered.

"Landmine, 0222, ready," Nathan spoke into the phone. He pointed to the pen and paper and motioned for me to get ready to write.

"011 32 488 12 19 37 . . . Yes, I have the code," Nathan answered as he looked at me to confirm I had the numbers.

I held them up so he could read them.

"Number confirmed; will stand by," he said and ended the call. Aubrey and I looked at each other, silently asking the obvious question: *What the hell was that all about?* But before we could ask it out loud, he slid the phone back to life and asked for the number. He dialed it and after a few seconds said, "28461201." He ended the call and looked over our way. "What?" he asked with a little playful smugness.

We looked back at him, wide-eyed and questioning.

"The number I dialed is a digital communications exchange service in Brussels, Belgium. It reroutes this number to a satellite that reassigns it to a different number. The second number was my pass code to access the DCE. We will receive a call in a few minutes that is untraceable. Well, that is not entirely true, but it's not traceable by anyone we're concerned with," he explained.

I was wondering who Nathan really was. *Landmine*... who the hell had and needed a *nom de guerre*? I guessed someone who was involved in things we were not supposed to know about. I would never be able to sit in another Historic Madison Morgan Foundation meeting and view him the same way. Of course, this thing was far from over, and I was assuming too much to imagine those future meetings would ever happen—at least with us there.

The phone rang to the tune of "The Devil Went Down to Georgia," which seemed apropos for our situation. Nathan gave me a furtive glance and answered it. He spoke the code into the phone. "24861201."

There was a brief pause. "I'm doing well, but by the nature and hour of this call, you can see I'm still keeping things interesting." He paused to listen. "It's a situation that's extremely sensitive, with national and international implications." Another pause. "No, I can't, but if you've been watching local or possibly national news, you are quite aware of the situation." He frowned. "Yes, they are aware and involved, but I don't think they know how bad things are or could get. Unfortunately, the lead agents are no longer with us." He listened for a while. "No, I don't think we have any choice. It will be something similar to our last operation in Darfur, and we can use the basic tactics and firepower we used there. One last thing: I'm involved in this with two civilians, and both will be a part of our team." Another pause. "I know, but these two have performed extraordinarily and deserve to see this to the end. I will be responsible for them." He looked serious as he listened to the answer. "We're at the Barrow County Airport in Winder, Georgia. . . . Okay, we'll expect you in about an hour." Nathan finished the conversation and ended the call. He looked over at us, knowing he owed us an explanation. He jumped right into it.

"Other than my wife, you two are the only civilians that know I was involved in more than managing land and picking up trash. After Vietnam, I was recruited and assigned to an intelligence operations group with the CIA. We were mostly part-timers, used for small, sensitive missions. Very rarely did we engage in anything dangerous—but we do have a few stories. Mostly we were diplomatic spies, and our missions lasted a week or less and were disguised as business trips," he explained. "I'm technically in semi-retirement—at least I was."

We were still silent and wide-eyed. Nathan shook his head and told us to stop gawking at him and go get some sleep. He walked over to a recliner and plopped down.

Never letting a good opportunity pass, I replied with a little chuckle, "Roger that, Landmine."

Nathan fell asleep in the recliner, but now that I knew he was a spy, I was sure he slept with one eye open. Eye open or not, he still managed to snore.

Aubrey and I curled up on the love seat, and it was a nice distraction from the perils of the day. With me behind her, we formed the shape of an S on the small sofa. The room was dark, and the only sensations were the feel of her soft hair on my face and the sensual aroma of her skin. Having nowhere else to put my arm, I wrapped it around her slender waist. She put her arm on top of mine. Our bodies were close—very close. I so wanted to talk to her and tell her the things I had waited so long to say, but she fell asleep. As she was sleeping, I lay there trying hard to think about airplanes, race cars, or something other than what was on my mind. It was Nathan's erratic snoring that interrupted the fantasy, and I finally drifted to sleep.

I could have only been asleep for minutes when I was startled by the sound of an inbound airplane. The pilot was changing the pitch of the constant-speed propellers, setting up for landing. I could tell by the sound that it was a twin-engine turboprop. It reminded me of a car commercial on TV from years back with two kids sitting on a porch, unable to see the cars passing on a nearby road. One kid was able to identify all the cars by their sound, but the other kid was not to be outdone. "Yeah, but what color?" he asked.

I didn't know the color, but I was certain the aircraft was a Beechcraft King Air 350I. Knowing the 350I was popular with militaries and governments, it did not surprise me that Nathan's accomplice would arrive in one.

Aubrey was still sleeping, and I did not want to wake her. I reluctantly removed my arm from her waist and looked over to see if Nathan had heard the airplane. He was not in the recliner, and I was not surprised.

Chapter Seventeen

The King Air 350I had already taxied to the ramp, and the high-pitched unwinding of the turbo-charged engines produced an intoxicating sound. I glanced around for Nathan but did not see him. The door to the cabin opened and was lowered to the tarmac. A shadow of a figure appeared in the dark and walked down the steps, aided by the pinpoint light from a small torch. Another figure exited the King Air and headed toward the rear of the airplane. With the help of the moonlight, I watched him as he walked, and I saw Nathan standing near the tail, waiting on him. Nathan's ability to keep secrets was becoming quite impressive.

I was a little disappointed to see Nathan's clandestine contact dressed in blue jeans and a heavy flannel shirt. I expected to see him clad in the stereotypical black suit, white shirt, and black tie. I would have even appreciated a trench coat and dark glasses. Like Nathan, he looked like, and probably was, someone's grandfather.

As I was paying attention to Nathan and his contact, I did not see the pilot slip into the darkness. He suddenly and silently appeared from behind me and stood at my side. I guess being cautious was protocol. He was dressed in a typical pilot's uniform with one minor difference: he had an asymmetrical lump underneath his left coat pocket.

"Good evening," he said with no offer of a handshake or introduction. He stood about three feet away with his feet slightly spread and his hands clasped in front of his waist. I could tell he was more than a pilot.

"Good evening," I replied. I wanted to ask about the King Air but could tell he was not there to talk. His eyes systematically scanned the airfield with keen alertness. We both stood there in a silence.

After about ten minutes, Nathan's contact walked back toward the cabin door and, without a glance, climbed back into the airplane. The pilot gave me a slight nod and returned as well. He pulled up the cabin door and, just as Nathan reached me, was spooling up the powerful engines.

"Let's go inside," Nathan instructed.

We walked inside to the smell of freshly brewed coffee. Realizing it was going to be a long night, Aubrey had three full cups waiting for us. She had switched on a light in the back room to provide more illumination than the glow of the computer screen. As we sat down at the table, I heard the King Air go to full power and the pilot release the brakes for a short-field takeoff. They were in the air by midfield, headed to wherever people like that go.

My attention turned from the airplane to watching Aubrey and Nathan make a production of adding artificial creamers and sweeteners to their coffee—trying to make it not taste like coffee. I sat there, a proud purist, waiting for them to finish.

After we all had a few sips, Nathan gave us a report. "So here's what's happening. As you can imagine, what we're involved in has hit the radar screens of every law enforcement agency in the country. Fortunately, it has not made it to the media . . . yet. Since it may have international implications, the CIA is working with the FBI. What's interesting is that with the explosion at the estate killing most of the people involved on both sides of this matter, the authorities have little information. Aubrey, you possess more info than anyone in the investigation. Colby, I guess you are next on the list.

"As soon as the FBI learns of our whereabouts, they're going to demand a debriefing. As of now, no one has made the connection between Mark, Dr. Lee, and the Braselton residence. My contact is going to locate the farm and initiate a reconnaissance flyover to determine if anyone is there. The airplane is equipped with heat detection devices that will show the heat signature of anyone in the house. If a signature is detected, we will immediately form a strike force and engage," Nathan explained.

"When do you think they are going to do the flyover?" Aubrey asked.

"I would say the request for the location and the order for the flyover were given before the wheels of the King Air left the ground. The flight from Dobbins Air Force Base will take about fifteen minutes and will provide real-time information to the analyst. The strike force is being formed as we speak."

"Wow, that's incredibly fast!" Aubrey exclaimed.

"As horribly inefficient as our government is on most things, security is not one of them. With the fluid exchange in real-time operations, we don't have the luxury of panels, focus groups, or bureaucratic red tape. If this operation is a go, we will know very soon," Nathan answered.

I only had one question—well, I had a thousand, but only one that mattered. "If they find the farm and they're there," I asked, "are we going to be part of the mission?"

"You're damn right we are!" Nathan emphatically answered. "Of course, the two of you won't be part of the assault on the house. For that matter, I'm sure all three of us will be located on the perimeter. Also, don't expect a phone call or any notification. If this thing happens, the team will show up, and we will have only minutes before we depart for the farm."

I looked over at Aubrey and could see that she was troubled. She silently got up from the table and walked outside. About a minute passed, and Nathan looked over at me and then at the door. My instinct said she wanted to be alone, but in matters such as this, my instincts had mostly failed me. I got up from the table and went to find her.

I saw her about twenty feet away, sitting against the side of the building. She had her arms wrapped around her legs and was huddled up with her head lowered to her chest. I stuffed my hands in my pockets and walked over and sat down beside her. She slipped her arm into mine and rested her head against my shoulder. I wanted to tell her everything would be all right, but I didn't know that it would. I stared out across the ramp at the long line of blue taxiway lights and tried to think past the last few days. What Aubrey had described before I had found her in the RV and what we had been through together after, felt like a work of fiction. It seemed far from reality that I was sitting there as one of the characters. I could feel she was struggling and wanted to talk.

"I can't stop thinking about all the horrible things that have happened," she said. "I feel like I'm in a spiral, spinning out of control. I feel so overwhelmed when I think about Mia and John and even that poor innocent housekeeper. I'm so scared this might never be over. What if we don't find him and he gets away? What would happen then?" Aubrey asked, gripping me tighter.

My mind drifted back to a conversation we'd had many years ago. "Do you remember once telling me how safe you felt with me?" I asked her. I knew I was going down the road of no return, but it was time to stop pretending. What we had might have been a hundred years in the past, but it was our first experience with love, and nothing could ever replace it. We spent many nights on the dock, talking about the future—our future. It didn't go quite like we had planned, but here we were many years later sitting on the tarmac at the Barrow County Airport. Over the past few days, it had felt like it had back then. We would fuss and fight, and then she would grab my hand and smile at me with her emerald eyes, and everything would be fine. No one could make me believe things were going to be fine like Aubrey could. I could feel her nod yes, and I continued.

"When you told me that, I was on top of the world. I knew what you meant by feeling safe: safe with the understanding that I would follow through with all that we had planned and protect you as well as your heart. I failed you back then. I guess I failed myself as well. But if you could possibly find the faith to believe in me again, I promise I will go to the ends of the earth not only to protect you but to gain your trust and show you how much I still love you," I said while taking hold of her hand.

Aubrey turned to face me and crawled into my lap. She stared straight into my eyes, studying me hard and cautiously, and I dared not move or say a word. Our eyes were locked, and she held the key to our future. It was almost unnoticeable, but I saw her look down at my lips and move closer. As my heart was wildly beating, our eyes closed and our lips pressed lightly together. I breathed her in, drawing her closer. I could feel my desire for her coursing through my body. Fueled with passion, I stood straight up, lifting her with me. She wrapped her long legs around my waist, and I turned and pushed her up against the building. We were no longer tentatively exploring. I kissed her hard and she responded. I pushed against her harder and our passion intensified. All the thoughts of the last few days were lost from our minds, but unfortunately, that did not last.

Headlights suddenly appeared out of nowhere, and we both knew what that meant. Aubrey slipped her legs down to the ground, kissed me once more, and walked toward the FBO. I walked a few feet behind her, and my mind was far from anything other than the vision that was right in front of me.

I wanted to grab Aubrey, jump into the airplane, and fly us far away from all the turmoil. We had survived incredible odds—especially Aubrey—and I didn't know how many chances we had left. I had just made some big promises, and keeping her safe was paramount. For all we knew, Mark could have an encore performance waiting at Dr. Lee's farm.

As we approached the FBO, we could see Nathan inside, talking to three official types. I was comforted to see they were dressed in what I had expected to see Nathan's contact wearing. We watched them through the window, and it appeared they were studying aerial maps of what I assumed was Dr. Lee's farm.

I touched Aubrey lightly on her shoulder. We made eye contact, and she followed my eyes as I looked over toward the airplane. "I think it's time we turn this over to them," I said.

She looked at the airplane and then back at me. She walked the two steps between us and hugged me. She put her head on my chest and held it there.

I wrapped my arms around her and pulled her close. I felt a strong sense of protectiveness and thought maybe, for us, this nightmare was over.

After about a minute, she relaxed her arms and pulled slightly away. She lightly put her hand on the side of my face and momentarily held it there. It was a sign of endearment and something else as well. She turned away and walked inside the FBO. She pulled up a chair and joined the others. I could see her talking, and it appeared she was asking to be briefed on the plan. She saw me still watching from the window and gave me a little smile. Without her going into a long explanation, the touch on my face had said it all.

I left the FBO and walked over to a small patio and sat down in an Adirondack chair. Leaning my head back, I stared at the immense sky. A broad swath of light humbled me as it always had. The Milky Way, our home and one of billions of galaxies, was a thousand light years in distance from our spot at the Barrow County Airport. The infinite and overpowering realm of the heavens seemed to proportionately simplify most worldly concerns. I realized Aubrey could not walk away. Throughout this ordeal, she had put her life on the line and seen her friends pay with theirs. She could have turned her back on this battle numerous times, but turning back now was not an option. If her decision was to stay to the end, so was mine. The three of us would see this through and pick up the pieces when it was all over.

As I was pondering this, more headlights appeared. Several black Chevrolet Suburbans quietly pulled onto the ramp. All the doors opened at once, and three assault teams in full combat gear efficiently stepped from the vehicles. They surrounded the three Suburbans and stood at guard. I heard the door from the FBO unlatch, and it was Aubrey.

She saw me sitting in the chair and walked over. She sat down next to me and gently squeezed my hand. "The reconnaissance flight found four human heat signatures in the house and two cars: one car located in the carport and one further up the driveway. As you can see, the assault team has arrived, and the plan is to strike within the next ninety minutes," she explained.

"That seems soon. How far is the farm?" I asked.

"It's 8.3 miles from the airport and 1.2 miles down County Road 37. The driveway is an unlit, single-lane drive and has a 3 percent grade from the road to the house. The front of the house faces northwest, and there is a seventy-five-yard line of hardwoods surrounding it. The house is two levels with a daylight basement. It has a total of sixteen windows and three exits," she reported with a slight grin.

"Well, you already sound like one of them. You might be recruited for real once this is all over," I replied, quite impressed. "How is our boy holding up in there?" I asked and looked toward the FBO.

"Well, it's apparent he's done this type of thing before. The guys in the suits are all huddled around him and asking questions. He seems to be in his element."

"What are the plans for us? Are we going to be in charge of the soup and sandwich line?" I asked sarcastically.

She responded with a small laugh. "No, but it's not much better. Like Nathan said, we are going to be observers—observing far from the action." She rolled her eyes.

I might not have been able to totally remove her from the scene but was glad to hear we were not going to be anywhere close to the house. If we could just get through that night, maybe it would all be over soon.

"Well, when you think about it, we've been surviving on instinct and reaction," I said. "These folks are professionals and have spent years planning and training for situations like this. I think it makes sense we take an observer's position," I explained, trying to be convincing.

"Really?" she asked mockingly, and then she lowered her voice. "I'm hearing this 'We should let the professionals handle it' from a person who dug a tunnel to a doghouse and set explosives around the perimeter of his house! You handled a team of assassins but are tentative about engaging Mark and Dr. Lee? I know what you're doing and I appreciate it, but I want to be right there when everything is final. I want to see the fear in Mark's eyes when he knows he's caught."

I knew she was right, and I agreed with her, but there's a time and a place for everything, and as much as I wanted to be part of the strike team, I knew it was time to let Nathan and his team finish it.

After a few minutes of watching Aubrey nervously tap her foot, I saw the door to the FBO open. Nathan approached us. "You two okay?" he asked.

"Yeah, we were just discussing the details of the plan. One of us is not too happy about our assigned position," I said and pointed a finger at Aubrey.

"I know," Nathan said, looking down, "but the bureau or the agency would not permit either of you to be a part of the actual assault, and I agree with them. These people have trained together and know each other's every move. Their lives depend on their ability to coordinate and communicate with no second guessing. They're equipped with the skills to instantly react to scenarios that cannot be predicted, and we, including myself, would be in their way. My expertise is in planning these responses, not being a part of the assault team. I'll head up communications and monitor the attack. You'll each be issued a communication device, and you can monitor the assault as it unfolds. Your devices will not be able to transmit, only receive," he explained.

As we were listening to Nathan, one of the group leaders approached us. "Mr. Roark, we are rolling in five minutes, sir," he reported and walked back to his team.

"Well, this is it. I never know how these operations will turn out, but I can assure you, if Mark is in that house, he will not escape," said Nathan. "In one short hour, this whole thing will either be finally over, or the nightmare will rise to a whole new level."

Chapter Eighteen

Headlights appeared from the around the corner of the FBO, and I was thinking, *Who now?*

It turned out to be another black Suburban and our ride to the Braselton farm. The driver got out and joined the others. He was dressed in the same black military-style uniform, and I assumed he was part of the assault team. Looking at the group, I was reminded of a professional sports team. They were all stretching or running warm-up drills, and I could note a slight nervousness, akin to pre-game jitters. Tonight's performance would have widespread ramifications; it would be much more than a simple win or a loss. Their success or failure would not be tallied by runs or points on a scoreboard—but by bodies removed from the scene. I was hoping our team was more prepared than our opponents and that the night would end in a shutout.

Aubrey and Nathan seemed to be relaxed and ready to engage in the unfolding event. I was far from ready or relaxed and felt somewhat apprehensive. We had been instructed not to carry any weapons, and that was not sitting well with me. I could only go so far in relinquishing control, and being stripped of basic protection was going too far. I understood we would not be near the engagement area, but I'd heard and seen what Mark was capable of and was not so sure we were safe anywhere.

I excused myself before climbing into the Suburban, explaining I had forgotten to lock my airplane. Of course, I had locked it and was returning to retrieve my Glock Model 19 from the baggage compartment. The Model 19 is a popular 9mm backup weapon used by USAF pilots and is very light and efficient for emergency defense. I slipped the small weapon into my boot and trotted back to the truck. The leg of my jeans bulged out a bit over the left boot, and I saw that Nathan noticed. He gave me a slight nod of approval as we all jumped into the Suburban. We were in the last of five vehicles departing the airport. I took one last look out the window at the vastness of the sky—*perspective*, I told myself. *Perspective.*

Leaving the airport, Aubrey sensed I was nervous and out of sorts. She gently took my hand and gave it a little squeeze. She intertwined her fingers into mine and I immediately felt better. I slid next to her and moved our clasped hands into her lap. I wanted to put my arm around her, but not at the expense of letting go of her hand. She slid a little closer and gave me a gentle, wonderful kiss, followed by her warm smile. It was her way of telling me everything would be all right.

Sitting in the back of the cop car with Aubrey, I wished the moment would last. After a while, I could feel the road turn from pavement to dirt and knew we had arrived.

Our driver, as well as the others, turned off the lights and slowed to a stop. We were still about half a mile from the house and would travel the rest of the way on foot. The group gathered together at the rear of our Suburban and prepared for the assault. Aubrey and I stood a few feet away and watched.

In a seemingly choreographed display, the team checked their weapons, ammo, infrared illumination, and communication systems. The three teams were designated Alpha, Bravo, and Charlie. Each team had four members with each assigned a number, the leader being number one. The Alpha team leader was Alpha-one; the Bravo leader, Bravo-one; and their Charlie counterpart was Charlie-one. Except in emergency situations, the team members would only communicate with the team leader. Only team leaders would communicate with each other. The reason for this protocol was that when the action intensified, the last thing they wanted was everyone talking, creating confusion.

As we had been told, Aubrey and I were given communication devices that were for receiving only. We put them on and could hear the teams doing communication checks. After about thirty seconds, the headsets grew quiet, and moments later, we heard Nathan's voice give the command to move toward the house. The teams dispersed down the driveway and within mere seconds had disappeared into the woods.

Team Alpha was to secure the three exits and sixteen windows. Most of the windows were near doors or located high up on the house. Team Bravo provided security and was charged with flanking the other two teams, preventing a rear or lateral assault. The area of focus appeared to be the house, but it was important to cover all the angles. Team Charlie would dispense tear gas canisters simultaneously at four strategic spots. Within seconds, the entire house would be engulfed in the vaporous gas, leaving anyone inside unable to breathe or see. Both teams Alpha and Bravo would remain at their positions, expecting an attempt at escape or maybe a rear advance.

The teams were set, and we heard the prearranged signal of a microphone click from the Alpha team leader, indicating that the assault was ready to commence. After the teams were in place, we moved down the driveway and were about two hundred yards from the house but well out of sight. I heard glass break as the tear gas was being shot through either the doors or windows.

We were all intensely listening for the commands of the team leaders when I felt Aubrey abruptly grab my hand, and I turned toward her. She gazed back with an expression of pure fright plastered onto her face.

Nathan was a few feet away and also noticed she was in distress. He pulled off his communication headset and approached her with concern. "What's wrong?" he asked.

She did not reply, just stuck her finger up toward the sky, pointing. That's when we all heard it—the thump, thump, thumping of a helicopter overhead. It was about a thousand feet over the house and in a holding position. We had heard her story about her recent experience with a helicopter and had seen the devastation of the explosion on the news. It now appeared that Mark again had been one step ahead of everyone.

Aubrey moved as if to run, and Nathan grabbed her and embraced her in a protective hug. "Aubrey," he said, "that's *our* helicopter! I didn't think to tell you and Colby it would be arriving at the beginning of the assault. I'm so sorry." He held on to her for a few seconds, and then she pulled away.

"Are you okay?" he asked with concern and compassion. She looked more tired and resigned than angry, and I was sure that he was regretting the oversight.

"I guess you never get used to that sound, do you?" she softly asked Nathan.

"No, you never do," he replied. In another time and place, Nathan had learned to associate helicopters with impending tragedy.

Aubrey walked back the few steps to Nathan and gave him a reassuring hug. I watched as they held on to each other, strengthening their bond through the simple sound of the helicopter rotor blades.

The traffic on the radios snapped us back to attention. The helicopter's pilot was announcing that only two heat signatures were being picked up in the house and both were dim. He also reported that the area and woods around the house were clear of any activity. You could hear a collective silence on the radios. I think everyone was expecting four heat signatures and wondered what had happened to the other two.

With this report, Alpha and Charlie teams breached the house, with Bravo still on security. With no hostile engagement, teams Alpha and Charlie began searching their assigned sectors. Alpha team searched and cleared the basement, making their way upstairs, while Charlie team searched the upper two floors. Charlie team was the first to report.

"Charlie-one to Charlie team, report clear."

"Charlie-two, clear."

"Charlie-three, clear." As we waited to hear from the last member of the Charlie team, I was thinking we had not heard any gunfire. Possibly, they had escaped just before we arrived. I was sure Nathan and Aubrey were thinking the same thing.

"Charlie-four . . . uhh . . . Charlie-four to Charlie-one, I think you need to come to the living room on the main floor, immediately."

"Charlie-one to Charlie four, wilco."

We glanced at each other, wondering what was happening. After a long minute, Charlie-one reported. "Charlie-one to all teams, report to the main floor of the house and stand by. Situation is stable. Charlie-one to Agent Roark, do you copy?"

"Agent Roark copy. Charlie-one, go ahead."

"Please report to the house and bring the observers with you; we have a situation that needs your attention."

"Roger, Charlie-one. Moving with the observers to the house," Nathan answered.

Without speaking, we rushed down the driveway and ran to the house. The lights were on in the living room, and I could see the silhouette of the teams standing in a small group. We entered the house from the side porch and walked into the den. As we approached the team, they separated to allow us a view of the room.

We all three stopped in our tracks. Aubrey put her hand over her mouth to stifle a gasp. I just stood there dumbfounded, and I wasn't sure of Nathan's reaction. There before us were the bodies of Mark and Dr. Lee. Both were positioned on the couch with their heads leaned back. Each had a single bullet hole centered in his forehead. Since they still had a slight heat signal, we knew they had not been dead for long.

It was over.

The emotions that each of us were feeling were probably indescribable. We would never again have to live in fear of Mark and his delusional ambitions. I glanced over at Aubrey, as she looked at the bodies, and she seemed to be locked in a trance, looking at Mark.

My thoughts transitioned from the reality of what was happening to what it really meant—we could return to our lives. I guess I should have been shocked, traumatized, or at least aghast, but I wasn't. Instead, I wondered if Aubrey and I could continue what we'd started now that this was over. It crossed my mind that the adventure and adrenaline could have been driving the emotions.

Without the drama and the danger, things might turn awkward between the two of us.

As the thoughts were running through my mind, I saw her expression immediately change to fear, and I knew something was wrong. We all watched as she walked over to Mark's body and looked closer. I then saw what had alarmed her. Mark's right hand had been severed and was missing. Aubrey turned our way with a foreboding look. The three of us knew what this meant.

It was not over.

Chapter Nineteen

A week or so passed, and things were not exactly back to normal, although we were no longer being chased by a madman and now felt fairly sure the world was not on the brink of destruction.

After Mark and Dr. Lee's bodies were found, the next few days were filled with constant interviews. We were debriefed by the CIA, the FBI, Homeland Security, and even the Washington County Sheriff's office. (The sheriff wanted to know a little more about the explosions at the farm.)

The number-one question that no one had an answer for was who had killed Mark and Dr. Lee. Of course, we had no idea who had killed them. Everyone involved in the case that Aubrey knew was likely dead. Neither Nathan nor I had ever come into contact with anyone involved—other than the people who had tried to kill us, and we'd failed to get their names. The worst fear was that someone on Mark's team might have had other plans for the virus and forced Mark and Dr. Lee to give up the H3N7-1.

If they were the other two missing heat signatures at the farm, and had gotten away with the virus, God only knows what could happen. All we could do was report what we knew and hope for the best.

The toughest interviews were about Mia and John. Aubrey was adamant about not destroying their character. The three of them had unselfishly thwarted the plan of destruction and had formed a strong relationship. She remained loyal to them, even in their deaths. She made it unequivocally clear that, if I knew what was best for me, I would keep my mouth shut about anything she had told me.

With my best Sergeant Shultz impression, I told her, "I know nothing! I see nothing!"

She recognized the reference and gave me a smile.

She had the same conversation with Nathan. However, I don't think she threatened him the same way she did me. His response was that he had worked his whole career in an industry filled with things implied and untold. He also told us not to worry about the interviews. Nothing that had happened would ever hit the light of day. Neither the CIA nor the FBI would ever admit that civilians were involved.

We finished the interviews and, after signing a few confidentiality agreements, were cleared to go back to our lives. We eased back into Madison relatively unnoticed.

The local paper ran an article about Nathan's condo being broken into and reported that there had been gunfire and windows broken but that there had been no arrests. The story said that Nathan and his wife had been in Florida when it happened.

No one had any idea I had returned from Paris, if they even knew I'd gone. Aubrey's mysterious return to town was trumped by a cheating scandal involving a couple of prominent citizens.

All in all, things had returned to normal fairly quickly. I was spending most of my time in Warthen, preparing to rebuild and repair the damage from the explosions. (Luckily, the sheriff is a good friend and accepted my story that I was dynamiting pine stumps.) The dogs were alive and well, and other than a little loss of hearing, seemed content and happy.

Aubrey was backlogged with work, and Nathan was busy with his foundation and "civic duties."

I think the three of us realized during the ordeal that life can and will change like the direction of the wind, leaving us unbalanced and unguarded. Sometimes it will be just what we asked for, and sometimes we'll find ourselves picking up the pieces. Whether it's a celebration or a challenge, we will always need the love and support of those close to us. We'd banded together and overcome incredible odds by trusting and believing in each other. The altruism we shared had renewed my belief that we were all capable of doing the right thing, even if it meant possibly losing our lives. Aubrey had all the reasons in the world to return home and not put her life in jeopardy—but she understood that fate sometimes puts people in situations that they have to see through no matter what the cost. Her risk was placing herself in peril to help save the world from a madman. In Nathan's case, he unselfishly helped a friend in need, plain and simple. As for me, I helped the one I loved.

It's true that most people will never be put to a test that gives them the opportunity to help others by making an unselfish life-or-death decision. But there are heroes who prove every day that the innate drive to help or save someone else is part of a person's soul and is what I believe gives us hope for the future.

As for Aubrey and me, sometimes love does not fail.

A few days after the interviews, we jumped in her new Jeep and took a trip to Jewell. Her mother and father had moved to Augusta, and the big house was only used on occasional weekends for family gatherings. We crossed the bridge at the shoals, and I could see the house prominently sitting on the hill. Aubrey gave me a smile and squeezed my hand. "It's been a long time, hasn't it?" she asked.

We drove up the familiar driveway and parked in the back shed. It seemed things had not changed a bit. Mr. Reese's 1940s Willys Jeep was parked next to the old Ford tractor, just as it had been the last time I was there.

We entered the kitchen through a side porch door and walked through the house without speaking. It too was just as I remembered. It had been thirty years, but it felt like I'd just been there the day before. We stepped back out onto the side porch and eased our way toward the steps leading to the river.

Hand in hand, as we had done many times, we walked down to the dock. Steam was coming off the water and covered most of the river. It appeared that we were standing in the clouds. I could feel the emotions from long ago collide with the present.

Sitting on the same bench where I had told her so long ago that I loved her, I told her again that day. She rested her head on my shoulder, and I put my arm around her. I held her tight and never wanted to let go. It reminded me of being sixteen and falling in love for the first time. I whispered that I would never let another day pass without telling and showing her how much I loved her. She is the love of my life—and will always be.

She turned toward me and I could see the tears flowing. In a soft voice, she said, "I've loved you since our first summer together and have never stopped. When I saw you in Madison, it was so hard to keep my feelings from you. I felt so helpless when I had to let you go before, and I knew I couldn't do it again. When I realized you still had feelings for me, I was afraid they might not be enough—just like in the past. It was the hardest thing I've ever been through in my life—not knowing. There was no way I could share the deep, wonderful love I had for you until I knew. With all my heart and everything that I'm made of, I now know."

Epilogue

I flew into Madison from Sandersville and was taxiing the airplane to the ramp when my phone rang. I looked down at the display. I usually don't answer phone calls when in the airplane, but it was Aubrey. I pulled to the side of the ramp and answered, "Yes?"

"Where are you?" she quickly asked.

"I'm at the airport," I replied.

"What airport?" she impatiently asked.

"The Madison airport," I answered. I'd spent the last week or so in Warthen and decided to fly up to Madison for a few days. I was anxious to see Aubrey and had decided to surprise her and not tell her I was flying in.

"I need to see you. Can you come by the house?" she asked.

"Well, well, well, it's only been a week," I said. "You must have read my mind," I added with a touch of confidence.

"Not that, you idiot. I have something I want to show you. Come over now!" she playfully demanded.

"I'll be there in twenty," I replied.

I arrived at her house, and she was waiting by the door. She gave me a quick kiss and headed toward the sunroom in the back. She seemed excited and was motioning for me to hurry.

"Come on," she said and led me back through her bedroom to the sunroom.

"What surprise do you have for me back here?" I asked, raising my eyebrows suggestively.

She just rolled her eyes as usual and picked up something from a side table. "This afternoon at work, FedEx delivered an unexpected package," she told me. "We were extremely busy, and I didn't get a chance to open it until just before I called you. You are not going to believe what it is!"

I couldn't imagine what it might be, but she was excited and couldn't wait to show me. She pulled a letter from the FedEx box and started to read.

Aubrey, my dear friend,

One of the most overwhelming and wonderful feelings of my life was the moment I realized you were alive! I cannot express the joy I felt upon hearing the news. After several weeks of being on the run, John and I have found a place where we feel safe and can start a new life.

I'm sure all kinds of thoughts have crossed your mind, and I want you to know everything that has happened—starting with the moment John and I ran from the foyer. We ran to the basement to check the safe. I was frantic, thinking Mark might have taken the H3N7-1. I could picture the door wide open and the virus gone.

We had just made it down the stairs when the house exploded. There were no charges in the basement, so the blast went up.

We were knocked to the ground, and the first floor caved in around us, but luckily we escaped injury. My first thought was of you. I wanted to go look for you, but it was clear the house was gone and no one could have possibly survived. We escaped the basement through a ventilation duct and ran south toward Moores Mill Road. We managed to find a taxi and made our way back to John's apartment.

I cried all afternoon thinking about you and how much you had sacrificed and how it was so unfair that you were gone. I vowed that afternoon to find Mark and anyone else responsible and make them pay.

We tried the entire next day to think about where Mark might have gone and came up with no answers. I went to bed early from exhaustion and had a dream about my mom. We were laughing and running through a field of sunflowers. I was probably nine or ten years old, and she was motioning for me to follow her. I could see she was leading us back to the house at the Braselton farm.

I woke up and went to the kitchen for a glass of water, and that is when I realized the significance of the dream. Mom had passed away before the purchase of the farm and had never been there. I immediately knew that Mark was at the farm and she was leading us there. I ran back to the room and woke up John. We discussed it and knew what we had to do.

We got dressed and made our way to the farm. If he was there, we had no time to lose. We watched the house until just after midnight and confirmed that Mark and Dr. Lee were there. I had the keys to the house, so we approached the side door to the kitchen and unlocked it. The alarm immediately started blinking, giving us only seconds to disarm it. I punched in the code, which was my birthday, silencing the alarm. We moved through the kitchen and into the den. Mark and Dr. Lee were sitting on the couch talking. I wish you could have been there to see the shock on their faces. Utter disbelief is an understatement.

I would like to say we had an engaging conversation on their epic failure, but Mark, with an expression of rage, reached for a gun. I had no choice but to pull my weapon and shoot him. I was looking at Mark when I caught a glimpse of movement to my right. I turned to see that my dad had raised a gun toward me and was about to fire. He had so much hate in his eyes, and I froze with the reality that he was going to shoot his daughter. Well, since I was not his flesh and blood, I don't think he really ever considered me his daughter.

I heard the shot but did not feel it. That is when I noticed a large, red dot on his forehead. John had saved my life and spared me a bullet from my father. He immediately ran over to comfort me, but there was no need. My father had abandoned me years ago and was already dead to me.

My immediate thoughts were about my mom. I knew that wherever she was, she would understand that I had done what I had to do. It ran through my mind that if she had not died, maybe we could have prevented this whole thing from ever going this far. I felt the sadness welling up in me but had to hold it back. I knew that one day it would all come crashing down on me, but today was not the day. Our mission was not quite over. We stood there looking at the two lifeless figures, and that is when the idea came.

H3N7-1, along with the H3N7, had to still be in the laboratory safe. The more I thought about it, Mark did not know the plan had failed until the house servant did not contract the virus. He was in San Francisco and could not have removed the parent H3N7-1. As hidden as it was, and underneath the rubble, I doubted the safe had been discovered. We had to get to it and destroy the virus, but there was only one way to access the safe. I remembered our conversation sitting at my condo table and pulled out my Randall knife. With no sense of guilt, I ran the sharp blade across his wrist and cut off his hand.

Since it was early morning and still dark, we rushed from the house to get to the estate before light. I later found out we'd only missed the assault team by minutes. We parked my car in a pull-off area on Moores Mill Road and took our previous path through the woods to the estate. We found our way through the rubble and entered the basement through the same ventilation duct. We had no choice but to use a flashlight and were fortunate there was no law enforcement in the immediate area.

John brought a small battery and power source and connected it to the wires leading to the safe. I pulled

Mark's severed hand from a small bag and placed it on the digital scanner. The laser had to pass it several times, and I had a sudden fear that I had cut off the wrong hand, then the green light appeared and a tone signaled that the safe had unlocked. I threw Mark's hand on the floor with total disregard.

As John unlatched the door to the safe, I held my breath. What if it was empty? With the door open, I pointed the flashlight into the safe, and there it was—a three-ounce vial of the H3N7-1 virus. Unleashed, it would reproduce and cast sickness and death upon hundreds of millions, but that was not going to happen. Its weakness was the same as the controllable H3N7—hydrochloric acid. It was harmless until activated by the acid, but I took great care in wrapping it and the remaining H3N7 vials in cloth and placed them in a small insulated bag.

We made it back to John's and had to wait a few hours for the stores to open. John ran down to the local hardware store and purchased the acid. We opened the container that held a gallon of the hydrochloric acid and poured the contents of the vials into the acid. There was a noticeable reaction as the acid consumed the virus. With no proteins to feed on, it perished and was gone forever.

Now that you know how everything turned out, let me tell you about John and me. We are stronger than ever and could not imagine being more in love. Our plans are to be married soon, and I wish you could be here to stand next to me. We are no longer in the United States, and it's probably for the best. We struggled with what to do, but neither of us wanted to take the chance.

In a few weeks, we're going to send a letter to our boss explaining everything from beginning to end. Hopefully, over time we can get things resolved enough to return home. Neither of us has the desire to remain in law enforcement, and we are excited about a new life!

I have a million questions for you! How did you escape the house? Where did you go? Did Mark or his men try to find you? And how was it that you were on the scene that night in Braselton? Needless to say, I was shocked to hear you were there. (We are still in contact with one of our friends at the agency and get limited information on the case.)

You are an amazing person, and I'm thankful that you came into my life. I look forward to one day sharing a bottle (or several) of wine and hearing what happened and catching up on life. John says hello to "Wonder Woman." He wishes you the best and looks forward to seeing you as well.

The three of us created an incredible team and formed a lifetime friendship. John and I will always treasure it.

Take care, Aubrey. We love you and are praying that you are at peace and happy.

Until we meet again,

Mia and John.

About The Author

James Campbell grew up in Atlanta and earned a degree in journalism from the University of Georgia. Although he'd planned to pursue a career in his field of study, he somehow got pulled into the vortex of the business world, but never lost his desire to write. After twenty-five years of building and operating multiple businesses, he decided to fulfill his longtime ambition to become an author. *Mandatory Role* and its sequel, *Mandatory Flight*, are both filled with action, adventure, and, most importantly, romance. In these fast-paced novels, James combines his love for flying, travel, racing cars, and the outdoors with the eternal hope that love might really conquer all. He currently resides in the Georgia towns of Madison and Warthen.

Website:
jamescampbellauthor.com

Facebook page:
facebook.com/
JCampbellAuthor

AMZN
GooGL
BKR
SLB
SBNY
ALK
GNRC
ARE

CPSIA information can be obtained
at www.ICGtesting.com
Printed in the USA
LVHW01s2157200218
567218LV00001B/2/P